A REBEL AT THE CHALET SCHOOL

gr. 9

A REBEL AT THE CHALET SCHOOL

Elinor M. Brent-Dyer

Armada

Dedicated to Kathleen and Vera Park with love and very many
thanks from Elinor

First published by W. & R. Chambers Ltd.,
London and Edinburgh.
First published in this revised Armada edition 1974 by
William Collins Sons & Co. Ltd., 14 St. James's Place,
London SW1A 1PS.

This impression 1983.

© W. & R. Chambers

Made and printed in Great Britain by
William Collins Sons & Co. Ltd, Glasgow

CHAPTER ONE

THE RAGGING OF MISS NORMAN

"HELLO, Joey! What's gone wrong now?"

Jo Bettany, seated in the Sixth form-room, looked up with a start as Anne Seymour came and sat down on the lid of her desk. "You, Anne? What makes you think there's anything wrong?"

"Your expression, my dear. If I were asked, I should say that something really desperate had happened. I hope everything's all right at the Sonnalpe?" she added inquiringly.

"Perfectly all right. I had a chat with my sister through the 'phone this morning—she's downstairs again, you know—and Babs is to be christened next Sunday. I'll have to remember to call her Sybil now, I suppose. The Robin was sent to bed early last night, and will have to go at eighteen for the whole week, by the way."

"*Robin?* What on earth has she been doing?"

A faint grin lightened Jo's gloomy countenance for a moment as she replied, "Mixing powdered chalk with the ink in the Second form-room. *Isn't* she coming on?"

"Well, she's got to the mischievous age," said Anne consideringly. "Eleven, isn't she?"

"Eleven last week. But *Robin!* I lost my breath when I heard."

"It's a good sign," said Anne. "She's evidently much stronger when she can be so much naughtier. I always think that very good children are generally too feeble to be anything else."

"Yes; there *is* that in it. But Robin's not been an angel all her life till now, by any means. She's been naughty on occasion."

"But what's gone wrong if it isn't the Sonnalpe?" persisted Anne, suddenly returning to the first question.

"Oh, just that little ass Joyce Linton has got into a row again."

"But what has it to do with you? And who is the row with, anyhow?"

"Miss Norman. You know, I do think it's a mistake to give her girls like Joyce and Thekla to deal with. Everyone agrees that she's simply marvellous with the babies, and they all adore her. But she simply hasn't an idea how to manage girls any older than ten."

"But why should she have anything to do with those two? They're both Lower Fifth."

"They are; but neither of them knows much French, and Joyce has next to no German. Thekla, of course, despises French, and Joyce, apparently, did *not* bother with it at her last school—little idiot! It must have been good there, because her sister isn't at all bad."

"I still don't see what all this has to do with Miss Norman. I wish you'd cut the cackle and come to the 'osses, Jo!"

"So I am if you'll only give me time. You see, Miss Norman was educated in France, and as she has a certain amount of free time, Mademoiselle evolved the brilliant idea of turning her on to all those who need extra French—people like Mary Shaw, and Enid Sothern, and Biddy O'Ryan, and of course, Thekla and Joyce. Well, as far as I can gather, Thekla and Joyce, who haven't relished being put with babes of ten and eleven, have done their best to brighten up the classes—from their own point of view. They've done precious little work themselves, and have taken good care that nobody else did any. Mary and Enid are imps, of course, and they and one or two of the others have followed the example set them by two Fifth Formers, and I can't say I blame them very much."

"Nor I. But how do *you* come into all this?"

"Well, they have one period when I'm free, and they work in that room at the end of the passage, next door to the library. This afternoon, I went along there to put in an hour on Spanish history. I hadn't been there long before I found I wasn't going to be allowed to do much work. There was the most awful noise coming from next door."

"What sort of a noise?"

"Oh, the whole lot, whoever they were—I didn't know then—were singing 'God Save the King' at the tops of their voices."

"*What?*" Anne looked startled at this. "But didn't the silly little asses *know* they'd be heard?"

"Who was there to hear them? The form-rooms are all at the other end of the house, and

7

there are only the stock cupboards under that room. They couldn't be expected to know that *I* was anywhere on the scene. The library isn't in use at that hour as a rule."

"I'd forgotten that. Well; go on!"

"Well, naturally I thought it must be some people who had no one with them, and I went in to tick them off thoroughly. I got a shock when I saw Miss Norman there, I can tell you."

"What was she doing?" asked Anne curiously. "Rather a horrid position for her, wasn't it?"

"Disgusting! Oh, she was saying, 'Asseyez-vous—tenez-vous tranquilles!' and looking awfully worried, poor thing."

"But—how feeble she must be!" said downright Anne. "I'd like to see them treating *me* like that—I'd soon show them their mistake!'

"Miss Norman is very jolly, but she's too soft to deal with criminals like Joyce and Thekla. Any other of the Staff would have jumped on them so heavily that they wouldn't have dared to say they were alive for the rest of the term. But she just doesn't seem to be able to manage it with them."

"Then why on earth didn't she report them to Mademoiselle? *She* would soon reduce them to flinders!"

Joey looked at Anne straightly. "Would *you* report them for behaviour like that if you could help—especially when you knew it would be tantamount to saying, 'Sorry; but they are absolutely beyond me'—*would* you, now?"

"I hadn't thought of that," acknowledged

Anne. "Well, what did you do after bouncing in on them like that? I know you *did* burst in, frothing with strange oaths—I know you, Joey!"

"You're quite right; I did. What did I do? Oh, said 'I beg your pardon, Miss Norman. I didn't know you were here.' What else could I say?"

"Nothing, I suppose. What did *she* say?"

"She said, 'I'm not surprised at that,' and glared at them."

"On the weak side, rather," commented Anne

"Of course. And the worst of it was that as soon as they saw me, the little brutes shut up and became like funeral mutes. Joyce went on humming abstractedly, and Thekla did it with —with—"

"With a glare of defiance?" suggested Anne "The wonder to me is that she condescended to sing the English national anthem at all! I wonder it didn't choke her!"

"Me, too," agreed Jo.

"Well, what happened next?"

"Nothing much. I didn't see how I could interfere—after all, she *is* a mistress!—so I just said that I was sorry again, but I heard them making rather a noise from the library where I was working, and then left the room."

"Any further efforts at a sing-song after that?"

"Not one. They might all have been dead next door for all the sound I heard. *And* I listened with all my ears!"

"Ah! They knew *you* wouldn't be soft with them," said Anne shrewdly.

"The worst of it is, it looks so pointed. I've kept out of Miss Norman's way since then, but I can't go on doing it for ever, and I shall feel such a fool when I meet her. And I don't suppose she'll be fearfully comfortable either. She must *know* that I realise what was up. And I can't possibly take any notice of it, dearly as I should love to give them what they deserve. It's up to her to keep them in order, and I can't very well go shoving my oar in. But this sort of thing can't go on, you know."

"She ought to report them," said Anne decidedly.

"I don't suppose she'll do that unless they drive her to it. As I said before, it's simply saying that she isn't capable of handling them, and I can't imagine that any mistress would like to own up to that. I should hate to do it myself!"

"Well, you're quite right saying you can't take any official notice as things stand. I should let it go at that for the present."

"All very well; but you're not head-girl, and I am. If that sort of thing goes on we shall be having the Juniors thinking it funny or clever to play up the mistresses *and* the prefects. We've never had much of that sort of thing here—just an occasional odd sinner. But this is more or less organised. I don't mean to let it get any hold in the School if I can help it.'

"I don't see how you *can* help. Head-girl or not, you can't go barging in on a lesson every time they misbehave. And you certainly can't

10

report them over her head. So what are you going to do about it?"

"I wish I knew. It's most frightfully difficult to know *what* to do."

"What is it that is so difficult?" asked a fresh voice; and Jo turned to see Frieda and Marie coming into the room together, followed by Simone Lecoutier and Vanna di Ricci.

"It's that little wretch, Joyce Linton, and the ever-sickening Thekla," said Anne. "Tell them, Joey."

Thus urged, Joey repeated the story she had told Anne, and the four prefects listened attentively.

"But what a state of affairs!" exclaimed Vanna when the tale was at an end. "And were they quiet after you had been in, Jo?"

"Deathly quiet," said Jo. "That's the sickening part of it."

Marie flopped dejectedly into the nearest chair "It is all very well for you who have nothing of which to be ashamed. But Thekla is my cousin, and—"

"Third cousin about ten times removed!" put in Jo hastily.

"Still, she *is* a relation, and it is *not* nice that she should bring such disgrace on us all. I wish she had never come here!"

"But she does not bear your name, so it is not quite the same thing," comforted Simone.

"Yes—that reminds me! I've always been going to ask you about that," said Jo, changing the subject gladly. "How is that, Marie? You told

11

us that you had a mutual great-grandmother. How is it that Thekla's name is Von Stift and not Von Eschenau?"

"My great-uncle Wolfram changed his name to that of an uncle of his wife because the old man left him his estates if he would do so," explained Marie. "Also, he became a Protestant for the same reason. Of course he had been brought up Catholic like the rest of us."

"What a horrid thing to do!" said Jo disgustedly. "I'm not Catholic myself, of course; but I do think to give up your religion just for money reasons is about the limit. Why, the Stuarts gave up the crown of England rather than change. You know what is said of them— that they gave up three crowns for a Mass."

"Uncle Wolfram thought nothing of it," said Marie. "Really, I suppose Thekla's name should be 'Von Eschenau und Von Stift,' but they do not use it.'

'I'm not surprised; life's too short for such a signature as that would be," said Jo with a grin.

"I am only thankful they do *not* use it," said Marie. "But it makes no difference to the fact that Thekla is my cousin, and that her behaviour is abominable. I thought she was improving at the end of last term, but she is as bad this term as when she first came."

"Oh, not quite," murmured Jo. "At least she has not tried to get exercise books by fair means or foul when she wants them. And she doesn't fly out at people as she did. Also, she can walk a little, and she couldn't do *that*."

"No; but she is rude and insubordinate," returned Marie, stumbling a little over the long word, fluent though five years at the Chalet School had rendered her English. "It is wrong that any girl of her age should behave so. She is sixteen now—nearly two years older than any of the others, and she ought to set them a better example."

"It would be much more to the point if *Joyce* set them a better example," said Jo. "After all, she has come from a decent school, and she must know what is done and what isn't. Thekla, from her own account, only had a governess who daren't say 'Bo!' to a goose."

"But tell me, my Jo," said Simone, "what are you going to do about this affair? It cannot be permitted to continue."

"I know that as well as you. But if you can think of a solution to the problem, you're cleverer than I am."

"Could not one of us always be in the library on Tuesday afternoons at that hour?" suggested Frieda

"Who besides myself is free then?" asked Jo blandly.

There was a blank silence. No one was, for it was the day when the Sixth had their drawing lesson with Herr Laubach. Jo had been exempted from drawing during the previous term, as she had no gift for it whatsoever. But even she could not always reckon on being free then. She had no set lesson for the period, but as a rule any mistress who was free at the time gave her a coaching in some subject. On this particular day, Miss Wilson should have taken her for geography, but had been obliged to retire to bed with neuralgia, and so the head-girl had been left to her own devices. But no one could be sure that that would happen again.

"I suppose," said Frieda, "that we could not —but no; I see that we certainly could not."

"What were you going to suggest?" asked Jo curiously.

But Frieda shook her head. "No; it is an impossibility."

"Couldn't you deal with them for having disturbed you, Joey?" asked Anne.

"And practically tell them that the mistress in charge of them didn't know enough to keep them in order? Oh no, thank you!" said Jo.

"Then we can do nothing?" Simone sounded, dismayed.

"Nothing; except keep an eye on them. If only Miss Norman would report them *once*, I believe it would settle them. But I'm afraid that's just what she won't do—unless, as I said before, they really drive her to it," said Jo.

In saying this, she was quite right. What none of the girls knew was that this was in the nature of extra coaching, for as it came out of Miss Norman's own free time, she received extra salary for it, and she was paying for the education of her youngest brother. There were four of them, of whom she was the eldest. The sister next to her was secretary to a bank manager, and was able to keep herself, but could help very

14

little. The brother who came next was at Oxford, kept there by scholarships, and help from his godfather. The youngest of the family was a boy of fifteen, a clever fellow like his brother, and Ivy Norman rejoiced when Mademoiselle Lepâttre had suggested that she should take over these extra classes, for the salary added to them meant that she could send Alec to the big public school where Geoffrey had been.

Their father had died two years before this, having succeeded in muddling away all his money, and Mrs Norman was a gentle, rather fragile woman, quite unfitted to cope with difficulties. When Ivy Norman had been appointed Head of the Junior School at the Chalet, with English as her teaching subject, at a very good salary indeed, the whole family rejoiced. This additional money had been a further cause for joy, and she felt that if she could possibly manage it, she must go on. With her own work among the Juniors, she did excellently. She understood the mind of the small girl, and kept her charges in hand easily. But when it came to older girls, she knew herself to be nervous and hesitating, and not very sure how to treat them. The chances are that no one would have discovered this if it had not been for Joyce Linton, for Thekla von Stift was no character-reader, and the twelve-year-olds who came for extra French had, up to the coming of Joyce, regarded Miss Norman with the awe that surrounds any mistress, even Enid Sothern and Mary Shaw behaving themselves well on the whole. But Joyce had been to a big school, and under all sorts and conditions of mistresses, and she had not been at the Chalet a fortnight before she had joyously grasped the mistress's weakness, and promptly began to play on it. People like Mary Shaw, Biddy O'Ryan, Emmie Linders, Enid Sothern, and even Sigrid Bjorneson, a small Swede, followed her lead, and those extra lessons had become a purgatory to poor Miss Norman.

It had been a nasty shock all round for them when Jo Bettany had marched in that afternoon. The people concerned with the sing-song wondered what she would do about it, for they felt fairly certain that Jo would never let such a thing pass. As for poor Miss Norman, she was bitterly ashamed when she thought how the very appearance of the head-girl had hushed the small sinners she herself had been incapable of silencing.

"What on earth did Jo want to be hanging about the library at that hour for?" grumbled Mary Shaw to Joyce after Kaffee und Kuchen.

"How on earth should I know?" snapped Joyce, whose conscience was uneasy. She had caught a glint in Jo's eyes when they rested on herself, a glint which she had not liked, and she felt very uncomfortable.

"Will Jo report us to Mademoiselle?" asked Sigrid with a slight shiver.

"Of course not! It isn't her business," returned Joyce. "Miss Norman was supposed to be looking after us."

Sigrid was silenced, and Joyce brightened up

a little. "Anyhow, it's never happened before, and there's only a fortnight or so left of term now, so I don't suppose it'll happen again. We'll hope not, anyway, 'cos I've got a ripping plan for our next lesson."

"What is it?" asked Emmie Linders, a very fair child of eleven, who always looked, so Jo declared, as if she had changed eyebrows and lashes with someone extra dark, for in her these features were black, which made rather a startling contrast with her flaxen hair and pink-and-white skin.

"Well, you know Miss Norman said this afternoon that we weren't fit to be in a civilised community?"

"Yes; but I did not know what she meant by that," complained Sigrid.

"Well, she meant that we were behaving like savages," explained Joyce. "As she thinks that, I vote we give her some jolly good reason for thinking it."

"But how?" demanded Mary Shaw.

"Behave like savages, of course."

"But—how can we?" Emmie Linders looked puzzled.

"Oh, you goop! How *do* savages behave?"

"They eat each other," said Enid Sothern unexpectedly. "You surely don't expect us to do that? If so, bags me *not* to be the victim."

"Ass!" said the exasperated Joyce. "I didn't say *cannibals*!"

"Well, but I do not know how savages behave," persisted Emmie, who was rather given to harping on one subject. "I have never seen any."

"Never read any stories about them either, I suppose?"

"I have read *The Coral Island*," said Emmie doubtfully. "But we cannot worship snakes, or—"

"Good gracious, I didn't mean things like that, you ass! Do have a little commonsense!" said Joyce rudely.

"Then what *did* you mean?" asked Sigrid, seeing that Emmie had taken refuge in offended silence at this.

"Why, when she asks us questions, let's pretend we don't understand—"

"But we did that before—three lessons ago," said Enid. "Don't you remember how mad she got?"

"I know. But we won't say it like that, of course. Savages talk with grunts and clicks—it says so in the Second Form geography. *We'll* talk like that!"

"I see!" Mary Shaw was nothing if not bright. "And we could squat on the floor like the Australians do at Correeborees!"

"I suppose you mean Corroborees," said Joyce, with a superior air.

But here, no less a person than Thekla took a hand. Hitherto she had been silent; but this was rather too much for her sixteen years. "*I* shall not sit on the floor. It is childish and undignified."

"Very well, then; don't! *You* can do a war-dance if you prefer it."

"What else could we do?" asked Emmie, forgetting her sulks at this brilliant idea.

"Why, we can *all* dance war-dances if it comes to that. And savages always go to sleep anywhere and at any time," said Joyce, who might be truly described as a "snapper-up of unconsidered trifles" when it came to general information, though she was bottom of her form in arithmetic, and never by any chance remembered a single date in history.

"What—go to sleep in the lesson? She'll be awfully mad if we do!"

"Who cares? She can't *do* anything; and she won't report us, for she never does," said Joyce optimistically. "And let's go with our hair all over the place."

"Oh, yes! And we can paint our faces, too," added Mary enthusiastically.

"But how paint our faces?" asked Sigrid.

"With our paint-boxes, of course. We've all got them."

"You may do as you like," announced Thekla briefly at this. "I find it childish and undignified, and I shall not do it."

"I wonder you condescend to come to the lesson at all!" retorted Joyce.

"I am not coming."

"What? Don't be a goat, Thekla! Of course you'll have to come. She'll only send for you if you don't, and if you don't come, then she's safe to report you to Mademoiselle. No Staff worth her salt would do anything else. Then you'll get into a fearful row without having had any fun, and that isn't worth while."

But Thekla was not to be persuaded. After all, she *was* sixteen in years, and in some ways she was a good three or four years older than that. This "rag" which Joyce and Co were so joyously arranging had no appeal whatever for her. Moreover, she objected to having to take any lessons with children as young as Mary and Sigrid and Emmie, and she felt that this would be a good opportunity to make a stand.

The result of all this was that the disgusted younger girls finally sheered off, leaving her to her own devices, and gathered together in a corner to plan further torments for poor Miss Norman, who looked forward to these extra lessons with real dread nowadays.

It was Thursday before the extra-French people had a chance to put their plans into action, for the Wednesday lesson took place next door to the room in which Miss Annersley was teaching literature in the Upper Fifth, and they dared not bring *her* wrath on their heads, even Joyce preferring to keep in her good books. Miss Annersley was one of the gentlest people on the Staff of the Chalet School, but when she was roused, her tongue cut like a knife, and she was famed for such punishments as she did give. But on Thursday, they were once more at work in the little room next to the library, and they had the additional satisfaction of knowing that none of the Sixth could interfere with them this time, for they had seen the entire band progressing to the laboratory for a lesson with Miss Wilson.

Accordingly, when Miss Norman, inwardly quaking, appeared at the door, she found her class all squatting on their heels on the floor, the desks having been pushed to one side. What is more, not a single girl looked even Christian! They had all painted their faces with the most startling effects they could manage, and had carefully dishevelled their hair, adorning it with such feathers as they could find. Joyce, perhaps, bore off the palm, for she had back-combed her golden locks till they stood out all round her head with amazing fuzziness. They had been obliged to keep on their brown tunics and shantung tops, but two or three people had wrapped themselves in their travelling-rugs, and Mary Shaw had rolled up her sleeves and painted her arms.

"Girls!" gasped Miss Norman when she had recovered her breath. "How dare you behave like this? Get up at once!"

This command was received with a volley of grunts, clicks, and hisses such as were never before heard in any civilised classroom.

"Do you hear what I say?" exclaimed the angry mistress. "Get up at once, and go and make yourselves respectable!"

For reply, Joyce Linton sprang to her feet, and began to leap about the room, tossing her arms in the air, and grunting all the time. For a moment Miss Norman wondered if she were in full possession of her senses. Then she knew that the child was merely behaving extra badly. It had only needed this to bring her to boiling-point. Whether or not she must give up the extra work with the extra pay, this sort of thing must be stopped at once. She went to the door, and when she got there, she turned round. Her face was white, and there was a glint in her eyes that alarmed one or two people who had not lost their heads quite so badly as the rest.

"I am going straight downstairs to bring Mademoiselle," she said. "You will all stay exactly as you are until she comes."

"Sorry, but I can't keep *this* position long," said Joyce flippantly, balancing on one foot, and raising the other to the level of her eyes, as she spoke.

Miss Norman said no more. She simply left the room, shutting the door behind her, and a dead silence followed on the sharp click that followed, telling them that she had turned the key on them.

"The mean *pig*!" cried Joyce. "She doesn't trust us one scrap!"

Two or three people, who had thought of making a bolt for it once the mistress's back was turned, looked rather shamefaced, and shuffled their feet. As for Joyce, she might be mischievous, idle, and impudent, but she was no coward, and she raged at this insult to their honour.

They were not imprisoned long. In five minutes' time, they heard footsteps coming along the corridor, and then the door was opened, and

Mademoiselle came in, followed by Miss Norman, who still had that queer, white look.

Of what came next, few if any of the girls cared to think when it was all over. Mademoiselle was very gentle as a rule, and governed almost imperceptibly. But on this occasion, she let herself go. Before she had half-finished with them, most of them were weeping bitterly; and if Joyce and Enid managed to control themselves, it was only because they both had an almost boyish hatred of tears. Finally, their sentence was pronounced. For the rest of the term every girl would be degraded to the form beneath her present one. They would go to bed with the Juniors, and would take all their meals at the punishment table. For the remainder of the week, they would be in silence—a terrible punishment, for it meant that they might speak to nobody but the mistresses at lessons, and nobody might speak to them. Finally, they would each receive a bad-conduct report at the end of term, and one or two people looked decidedly blue over this. Emmie Linders, for example, knew that her father would be exceedingly angry with her, and Biddy O'Ryan, whose reports always went to Miss Wilson as Captain of the Guides, howled like a lost dog.

"And now," concluded Mademoiselle, "you will each one of you in turn apologise to Miss Norman for your disgraceful behaviour, after which you will go to your dormitories, where the prefects will come to you and see that you make yourselves clean and tidy again. When that is done, Thekla von Stift and Joyce Linton will come to me in the study, Thekla coming first." Then she looked round to fix Thekla with a glare, and discovered, what she had hitherto been too much upset to notice before, that Thekla was not there.

"Where, then, is Thekla?" she demanded. "How is it that she is not with the class?"

There was a dead silence. The Middles were indignant because Thekla had withdrawn from this last "rag," but they were not prepared to give her away.

"Was Thekla here before you came for me, Miss Norman?" asked Mademoiselle, turning to the mistress.

Poor Miss Norman, who could scarcely have told if the entire Sixth Form had been there, such was the turmoil in her mind, shook her head. "I'm afraid I don't really know, Mademoiselle."

"Well, I can understand that you were too much shocked at the wicked and unladylike behaviour of these children to notice," declared Mademoiselle. "They will, of course, apologise to you at once. I am ashamed to think that Chalet School girls could behave so badly. But I must know where Thekla is—Joyce Linton, do you know?"

"No, Mademoiselle," said Joyce, thankful to be able to answer this truthfully.

"Did you know that she was not coming to the lesson?"

Silence! Joyce was not going to tell a lie; neither was she going to tell tales. But Mademoiselle had already passed on, and was looking at Emmie Linders.

"Emmie Linders, do you know where Thekla is?"

"I think she may be in her dormitory," sobbed Emmie, who was still overcome at the thought of that bad-conduct report that was to go home.

Mademoiselle turned to the door and opened it. Frieda Mensch was passing just then, on her way to the library. Mademoiselle called her, and bade her seek Thekla von Stift, and when she had found her, to send her to the study at once.

Opening her eyes widely at the sights she glimpsed through the open door, Frieda gave up her quest of the book she had been sent to fetch, and ran off to seek Thekla. She finally ran her to earth in the Third form-room, where she had no right to be. She was also reading a novel the cover of which told Frieda that it must have been smuggled into school.

"You are to go to Mademoiselle at once," said the second prefect curtly. "She is in the study. And when you get there, you may report yourself for being in the Third form-room, and also for having that book at all."

"And if I do not?" asked Thekla, arching her brows insolently.

"Then I shall report you," said Frieda.

"Ah yes; you will tell tales," sneered Thekla.

But Frieda was not given to losing her temper, and she took no notice of the sneer. "Do as I bid you, Thekla, or you will be in trouble," she said. Then she added significantly, "I think you are that already, so it will be as well not to add to it."

Thekla coloured furiously, but something in Frieda's quiet gaze silenced her, and she went off to be sharply catechised and severely lectured on her rudeness to Miss Norman. She soon found that the fact that she had taken no part in that afternoon's affair availed her nothing, since she had calmly absented herself from the lesson without permission. The report she was obliged to give of herself, thanks to Frieda, made matters worse, and Mademoiselle had never bettered the lecture she administered then.

Finally, Joyce, who after half an hour's struggle had reduced her hair to something like its normal appearance, arrived, and was closeted with the head-mistress for nearly an hour. When it was over, she disappeared, and no one saw anything more of her that day. Whatever it was Mademoiselle had said to her, it seemed to have taken effect. But when she appeared next morning her eyes were so red and swollen with crying, that it was difficult to recognise pretty Joyce Linton at all. On the Sunday, she and Gillian had a long talk together, from which Gillian emerged looking very subdued, and Joyce had plainly been crying again.

As for the rest, they went about like mice all the rest of that week. And as long as they had to take those extra classes, they were the most diligent set of pupils the Chalet School had ever known.

CHAPTER TWO

A FRIEND IN NEED

IT was Sunday afternoon, and the Staff, freed for the time being from cares, were sitting in the salon at the Chalet School, drinking after-luncheon coffee, and managing very comfortably to forget that they *were* Staff.

Miss Stewart and Miss Wilson, closest of friends, were having an argument as to the best club to use when caught in the bunker at the ninth hole of the golf-links Dr Jem had had laid out on an alm a little higher than the Sonnalpe alm itself. Mademoiselle Lachenais and Matron Lloyd were discussing frocks, and little Miss Nalder, sitting near them and enjoying her cigarette, was putting in a word every now and then. Miss Annersley, curled up in a big armchair, was reading one of the "More William" stories, and punctuating it with chuckles, while Miss Leslie and Mademoiselle Lepâttre exchanged views with Miss Edwards and Matron Gould from Le Petit Chalet on the latest novels. Mr Denny was manipulating the wireless, and his sister and Miss Norman were discussing what they should do with the week's holiday which was so near.

"Personally, I'm thinking of going to Vienna," said Miss Denny, as she lit a cigarette. "Of course, if there's any likelihood of further political trouble, I'll have to give it up. But if the coast remains clear, I rather fancy that is what I'll do."

"I'm going up to the Annexe to spend it with Juliet Carrick and Grizel Cochrane," said Miss Norman, who had more or less got over the mid-week trouble by this time. "Can't afford to go anywhere very expensive, and it really isn't worth it for a week. We shall have a long summer holiday, thanks to this new arrangement, and I'm going home for that."

"What's that about going home?" asked Miss Annersley, closing her book with a final chuckle. "What a kid! How she thinks of all the things, I can't imagine!"

"How *who* thinks of *what* things?" demanded Miss Denny, taking the book unceremoniously from her. "Oh, 'William'! Yes; he is rather a priceless youth, isn't he?"

"Have you finished with that book, Hilda?" asked Miss Wilson from across the room. "I'm next for it, remember."

"Not quite, but you can have it this afternoon if you like. I'm on duty with the Seniors, and as it's such a glorious day, I'm going to take them out. Anyone know what the time is, by the way?"

"Nearly half-past fourteen," said Miss Nalder with a glance at her watch.—"Mademoiselle, that clock of yours is ten minutes fast. You ought to give it to Evvy and Co to boil."

A laugh went round the room at this reference to the antics of those young ladies in connection with the school clocks. It would be a long time before any of them were allowed to forget that particular prank which had taken the fancy of the whole School hugely.

"I prefer to wait till Gluckstein can come up from Innsbruck," said Mademoiselle Lepâttre placidly. "But you are right, my dear Hilda. Such a day as this is perfect for a promenade."

"I think I'll take the Middles off, too," said Miss Stewart, jumping to her feet as she spoke. "Coming, Nell?"

Miss Wilson—whose Christian name happened to be Helena—nodded. "It's my free Sunday, but I don't mind if I do. If I stay here I shall only stew over that idiotic book of Hilda's, and I haven't been out to-day except to go to church, and you can scarcely call that 'out.' All right, Con; I'll come."

"I think the Juniors had better have a walk, too," said Miss Edwards, rising also. "But be it known to all here present, we are going alone, as we have a secret to discuss for the Sale of Work. So don't offer to come, anyone, please."

"You and your secrets!" said Miss Nalder scornfully. "Miss Norman and I are going round the Dripping Rock, anyhow, so you can take your precious babies wherever you like. *We* shan't trouble you!"

They went off laughing, and Miss Edwards departed to seek her beloved Juniors and walk them up the valley towards the opening to the great Tiern Pass, where they all chattered hard about the secret that was thrilling them.

Meanwhile, Miss Annersley went to collect the Seniors and suggest that they should take a walk round the foot of the lake, and turn down to Torteswald, a little hamlet on the far side of the railway line that runs between Seespitz down to Spärtz.

"Good!" said Jo, who was standing at the door when the mistress came to seek them.

Gillian, who had been very quiet, and had looked thoroughly unhappy since the morning, looked up. "Will you be my partner, Jo?" she asked quickly.

Two or three people turned and stared at her, and Simone Lecoutier flushed pink. She was always inclined to be jealous where Jo was concerned. Five years before, when the school had just started, she had begged for Jo's friendship, and had, in the beginning, made herself wretched, and Jo irritable, on many occasions by her resentment of any other friends the head-mistress's young sister might have. However, Jo had taken a firm stand and insisted that she had a perfect right to have as many friends as she liked, and the French girl had slowly come to recognise the fact that the only way to keep the girl she admired was to share her. All the same, sensible as Simone had grown during the years which had passed, she still felt it if Jo went off with anyone fresh. Frieda and Marie were old stories, and the four of them made up a little coterie which worked together quite well. But Gillian was new this term, and Simone didn't like it.

"How quick you are, Gillian!" cried Frieda

before the French girl could say anything. "I'll be just as quick and ask Simone to be *my* partner."

"And I will take Carla," laughed Marie who had a great fondness for quiet Carla von Flügen. "Will you accept me as partner, Carla?"

Carla nodded, and Simone, thus recalled to the fact of her eighteen years and her dignity as a prefect, held her tongue—which was just what Frieda the peacemaker had intended. They all ran upstairs together to get their hats and coats, and were presently standing in the front path which only they might use, waiting for the mistress. As they stood in rank, Gillian turned to Jo with a face of such desperate earnestness as surprised the elder girl.

"Jo, when we break rank will you come with me?" she asked in an undertone. "I want to ask your advice.—I simply *must* talk it over with somebody!" she added desperately.

Jo looked her surprise. "Of course, if you like," she said slowly. "I don't know whether I shall be able to help you, though. You ought to go to someone with rather more commonsense than I have if you want advice," she added with a laugh.

"No; I'd rather ask you, and I'm sure you can help me," said Gillian.

"Oh, all right, then. We'll go off by ourselves, once we break rank," said Jo easily. She liked what she had seen of Gillian. To her eyes, there was in the girl the right stuff to make a leader in the school in the years to come. And they were coming very quickly. This was her own last year. In November, she would be eighteen, and she knew that she could not stay at school for ever. The end of the summer term would see the departure not only of herself, but of Marie, Frieda, Sophie, Carla, Eva, Vanna, Bianca, and Simone. There were several girls who were now in the Sixth who would be ready to step into their shoes, such as Anne Seymour, Louise Redfield, and Thora Helgersen. But after them must come the people now in one or other of the Fifths, and Jo felt that if Gillian Linton were still at the school she would make a very good prefect. Therefore, she prepared to listen to what she had to say.

"I only hope it's no bad news of Mrs Linton," she thought as they promenaded round the lake towards Seespitz which held the terminus to the mountain railway, a large "Gasthaus" or hotel, and one or two shanties where the railwaymen lived during the season when the railway was open.

It was not till they had turned to cross the water-meadows and the Gasthaus was left behind that Miss Annersley gave the signal for them to break rank; but when she did, Joey slipped an arm through her partner's, and drew her to one side, clearly intimating that they didn't want any of the others to join them. Simone saw, and her mouth took a pathetic droop. But Frieda called to Marie and Carla to join them, and they were soon busily discussing Baby Sybil's christening, and Simone managed to forget her troubles.

Meanwhile, the two walking alone were going in silence. Gillian was not very sure how to begin, and Jo, with no idea what it was all about, could not help her. At length the Fifth Former made a desperate effort, and broke straight into the middle of things.

"Jo, I'm in dreadful trouble, and I want your help—it's about Joyce," she added.

Joey cast a side-glance at her. "Oh? Well, I'm jolly glad it's not what I was afraid it might be," she said enigmatically.

"You mean—Mummy?" said Gillian in startled tones. "Oh, no; she's getting on quite well. Dr Jem told me so when he was down yesterday. If this warm weather continues, they are going to take her bed out to the balcony every day for a while. He thinks she's strong enough to stand the being moved now. Oh, it isn't Mummy!"

"No; so I see. But, Gillian, I don't see how you can be exactly responsible for Joyce's monkey-tricks. After all, she's fourteen—quite old enough to know what's done and what isn't. That last affair of hers really was the limit, you know. She's deserved every bit of her punishment. They all have, as far as that goes."

"I know. But—you see—" Gillian gulped for a moment. Then she went on, "You see—it doesn't—stop there for Joyce."

"Good gracious! What else? I should have thought she'd got a swingeing punishment enough for anything this time!" ejaculated Jo.

"She isn't to have any further punishment for this affair," said Gillian slowly. "Only—Mademoiselle told her that if she were reported for anything more this term, she couldn't be allowed to come back."

Jo was speechless for a moment. So bad a thing as this had never happened before. They had had insubordinate girls at the Chalet School before Joyce Linton. Grizel Cochrane had caused endless trouble during the early part of her sojourn there; and Cornelia Flower had not borne the best of characters at first, though she had certainly reformed considerably. Even Stacie Benson had been a good deal of a problem, though *her* fate had been decided by her own silliness. But never before had it been suggested that any girl behaved so badly that she must be sent away.

"She surely hasn't been as idiotic as all that?" said the head-girl at length. "I know she's got into endless rows; but goodness! we all do at that age!"

"But not rows like Joyce's," said Gillian, more composed now that she had got the worst of the telling over. "She proposed that feast that made her so ill. And the ragging of Miss Norman was her idea too. And Mademoiselle told me to-day that all the Staff complain that she is idle and disobedient and rude, and some of the younger ones are following her example. You know, Jo, she's my own sister, but I've got to say it—she *is* very pretty and taking, and all that, and the girls *do* follow her. They always did. It was the same thing at the High School. She's always been frightfully popular."

"Oh, I can guess that," said Jo. "She's a picture for looks, of course. And I know she's got pretty manners, and can talk prettily when she likes—not that she's ever wasted any of it on me," she added with a grin. "I can see that lots of the others would rally round her; but I didn't know it was as bad as all that."

"I've always known she was a little slacker at lessons," said Gillian. "At home it used to take me all my time to get her to do enough prep to keep out of any fearfully bad rows. Here, of course, I simply can't do it. We do prep in our own room, and she's with the rest of the Middles. That's just the worst of it, Jo. She has no one to stand over her and *make* her do her work if she doesn't choose to do it."

"My dear girl, there's always someone on duty."

"Yes; but you don't go round and prod them on, and say, 'Have you done your Latin?' and insist on seeing their French so that you can point out any *ghastly* mistakes, and hear her over her history."

"Mean to say you did all that in England?"

Gillian nodded. "Of course," she said simply. "Mummy was never strong enough to bother with it, so I had to."

"I don't see when you got time for your own work."

"Oh, I managed. For one thing, I've got the kind of memory that makes it easy to learn. And then I got so that I could do things quickly and accurately. It really is largely the result of practice."

"I don't know so much about that. No amount of practice would make me accurate as a geneneral rule," said Jo with an infectious grin. "They all say that there's no monotony about my efforts, anyhow. For if I get a thing right twice running, it's safe to be weirdly and impossibly wrong the third time!"

Gillian smiled faintly. "Well, I found it easy enough. But Joyce has always hated work of all kinds, and if she wasn't made to do it, she would never have learnt anything."

Jo was silent. Herself a very much younger sister, she had never had to cope with this sort of thing. And all the elder sisters she had ever known had left their juniors to look after themselves and expected them to stand on their own feet. To her mind, Gillian seemed to have nursemaided Joyce all along the line.

"I suppose you think I've been horribly selfish about it since we came here?" queried Gillian anxiously. "I know I should have thought more about Joyce—I can't think what made me forget her like this. I suppose it must have been partly Mummy's illness, though that's no excuse, really."

Jo found her voice. "If you want to know," she said bluntly, "I think Joyce is a jolly lucky babe to have had you behind her like this. At the same time, it couldn't go on, of course. She's fourteen now, isn't she?"

Gillian nodded, her sapphire-blue eyes fixed eagerly on Jo's face.

"Well, at fourteen, she ought to be standing on her own feet, and I think you'll have to let her. Oh, I don't say you oughtn't to keep, say half an eye on her doings. But you simply *can't* go on playing sheepdog to her all her life. For one thing, it's not giving her any chance to show what she's got in her. For another, it's not fair on you."

"But, Jo, you don't understand! You may think I'm an idiot, but hand of honour, Joyce isn't really fourteen in anything but age. She—she's just a *little* girl, not much older than your Robin."

"Not as old in some ways, I should think," said Jo crisply. "Even the Robin has sense enough to know that you can't rag a mistress as that crowd did without getting into scaldingly hot water. But look here, Gill, don't you think that the very fact that Mademoiselle talked like that to her will have given her such a shock that she'll try to pull up?"

Gillian was silent. Joey, looking at her, saw that she was horribly worried, and wondered To her mind, the bare threat of being sent away from the school should be enough to make any girl, however wickedly inclined, behave herself decently for the rest of her school career. For the first time the head-girl wondered if there were wheels within wheels of which she knew nothing. Subconsciously, she noted how pretty Gillian was with her black curls rippling round

37

her face and floating over her shoulders in two tails; with her pink-and-white skin, like apple-blossom; and with her very blue eyes beneath the long black lashes.

"Quite as pretty in her own way as Joyce," thought Jo. "And a heaps more interesting prettiness. Joyce is nothing but a fairy-tale-princess picture; but Gill has a good deal in her, behind her lovely colouring. I wonder what's at the bottom of all this?"

Then Gillian spoke. "I think it may have given her a lesson—I hope so. You know, don't you, Jo, that such a thing might—might—would upset Mummy very badly?"

"Does Joyce know that?"

"I said something about it this morning when —when we were talking. I don't know if she took it in—you see, I don't want to make her unhappy about Mummy, and she never has realised just how—how bad it's all been."

"Look here," said Jo abruptly, "what about *me* having a talk with her? Is she still in silence —oh, but she can't be if you've been talking to her."

"No; the silence ended last night," said Gillian.

"Then shall I see what I can do?"

"Joyce may not listen to you. You see, Jo, you *are* a pree—head-girl at that. And kids of Joyce's age always look on the prees as mortal enemies and something miles away from ordinary folk."

"It always seems to me such a mad thing," said Jo. "Of course, when I was a small kid at

38

Taverton High School—before we came here, that was—I know the prees seemed *aged*! But I'm not so awfully much older than Joyce, and we aren't nearly so inaccessible as they were."

"I guess you seem so to the kids here," said Gillian shrewdly. "Still, Joyce rather admires you at a distance—I know that from things she's said. For one thing, you're the only English prefect here. For another, you are so awfully fair—not that the rest aren't. But—well, Joyce does think an awful lot of you at the bottom of her heart."

"Oh, rot!" said Jo uncomfortably.

"It isn't rot—and I'm surprised at you for using such language!" Gillian was beginning to feel happier. Jo was proving herself a real friend in need. "Will you really talk to her, Jo?"

"Of course! Hello, we seem to be turning Come on and join Marie and Co. We've discussed this enough for the present. All the talking in the world won't alter things at present. I'll try and get hold of Joyce some time during the week and see if I can make anything of her. Don't worry, Gill. The kid will probably pull herself together after this last fussation. I've seen it happen before!"

CHAPTER THREE

JOEY KEEPS HER PROMISE

"JOYCE—Joyce! Are you doing anything just now?"

Joyce Linton stopped in her aimless walk round the playing-field, and looked round. Jo Bettany was coming up with her, her flushed face and tossed hair showing that she had been running. Joey's black mop was cropped page-fashion, with deep fringe in front, since it would have cost a small fortune to keep her in slides or clips. Even so, it was rarely tidy, and at the moment it looked like a golliwog's wig.

"Are you doing anything just now?" repeated Jo. "Because if not, I'm going round to the Post Hotel to get some stamps, and if you'd like to come with me, you can. I asked Mademoiselle, and she said it would be all right. Will you come?"

Joyce's face, which had been gloomy before, lightened a little at this, and she nodded. "I'd love to come if you're sure it'll be all right. May I really?"

"Rather! As long as Mademoiselle knows where you are, it's quite all right. You can always go out with a prefect providing you've got permission first. Come along and get your hat. I don't think you need bother about a coat; it'll be warm enough in our blazers."

Joyce nodded. It *was* a warm day. April had opened with varying fits of sunshine and rain; but for the last week the rain had gone, and only the sunshine remained, and the girls found their blazers quite warm enough even in the fresh breeze that was blowing. The pair walked decorously across the field to the school to get their hats and gloves. Then, duly attired, they went down the hall, and out by the front door which Joey, by right of her head-girlship, might always use. They passed the door of the Lower Fifth on their way, and just as they reached it, Thekla von Stift came out. She started when she saw them, and then glared at Jo, who took no notice of her, being engaged in struggling with a glove-button. Joyce flushed, and looked hurriedly away. She was not anxious to have any more dealings with Thekla than she could help in these days. But already Jo had finished with her glove, and was opening the front door.

"Come along, Joyce. Thank goodness the head-girl can use this, and not have the long trail round by the side door and the gate in the fence! It's one of the few—sadly few!—advantages of being head-girl!"

Joyce smiled, but her face was grave almost at once. They shut the door behind them, and went down the broad, flagged path, between borders already filled with blossoming flowers. Daffodils and hyacinths were nearly over; but tulips and white narcissi tossed their heads in the wind, and red and golden wallflowers perfumed the air deliciously. Near the gate lilies-of-the-valley were swaying closed green bells, that would open shortly and scatter their incense round. The garden was hedged round with sturdy, flowering bushes, all in bud, and outside these there was a stout fence of iron stakes and withies over which climbing plants were already throwing a delicate green veil. Jo swung open the gate in the fence, and she and Joyce went across the plank bridge which crossed the wide, deep ditch which had been dug all round the estate as a precaution against any flooding by the stream which ran across the alm, and which was subject to floods in thaw-time. Directly before the girls lay the Tiernsee, blue as a sapphire, with tiny waves, crested with pearly foam, and glittering in the sunshine. The birds were singing, and everywhere there were signs that spring had arrived with all her court.

Joyce turned and glanced across at the great mountain up the slope of which lay the shelf known as the Sonnalpe. From where they stood it was impossible to see the village; but she knew where it was.

Joey followed her wistful gaze, and her face became graver. "Better news this morning, though, Joyce," she said gently.

Joyce nodded, her face still sombre. "I know. But it's pretty awful. I thought Mummy was going on so well and would soon be quite fit again."

"She's bound to have some ups and downs,"

said Jo, still in that curiously gentle tone. "Try not to worry, old thing. At bottom, she *is* better. Only it will take time before she really gets on to her feet again."

Joyce said nothing. She had had a nasty fright on the Monday of that week when a telephoned message from the Sonnalpe had told her and Gillian that their mother had had a slight attack of haemorrhage. Mademoiselle had broken the news as gently as she could, softening the details as far as she dared. But Mrs Linton was still in too critical a state for them to leave her daughters in ignorance, and Joyce, with that heavy load on her conscience, had been bitterly unhappy about it. But this morning had brought the news that she was stronger, and there had been no return of the haemorrhage, and the doctors thought it only meant a temporary set-back.

Jo had been very busy all the rest of that Sunday when she had promised Gillian to talk to Joyce; and since then, she had thought it best to let matters slide till they saw how Mrs Linton went on. But now that the two days of anxiety were past and Dr Jem had 'phoned down that morning that his patient was once more making steady progress, she felt that she ought to fulfil her promise. Hence her invitation to Joyce.

She said nothing about it at first. Indeed, until they had been to the little shop built below the Post Hotel, which served the purposes of post office and general stores to the lake-folk, she chatted about school gossip— Cornelia's brilliant construe of *Festina lente* as "a Lenten festival"; the netball match they were to play against St Scholastika's on the coming Saturday, when they hoped to get their revenge, the Saints having defeated them by nine-seven in the last match; the milk puddings which had been the production of the Fourth on their last cookery day, and which they had forgotten to sweeten.

But when she had got her stamps and two bars of milk chocolate, she turned to her companion and said, "What about a stroll to the Dripping Rock? I said we might go when I asked leave, and Mademoiselle said we could so long as we weren't late for Kaffee und Kuchen. You haven't seen it yet, have you?"

"No," said Joyce, looking interested. "Some of the others have told me about it, though, and I'd love to see it."

"Right, then. We'll promenade along and take a squint at it. It ought to be simply shooting just now after all that rain last week. Here, take this; it'll be something to nibble as we go. This weather always makes me ravenous, and I should imagine it has the same effect on you."

Joyce took the proffered bar of chocolate, and together they went along the lake-path, munching amiably. Jo strolled along, her hands in her pockets, her hat on the back of her head. Once or twice she broke into a clear fluting whistle, but she always checked herself.

"It's a terrible thing to have a temptation to whistle on all occasions, Joyce," she said once.

"But you do it so beautifully," said Joyce, who

was totally unable to manage anything like a whistle herself. "It sounds like a blackbird."

"I dare say; but it's very strictly verboten—in term-time, anyhow. Only I keep forgetting, and it's so easy to forget sometimes, as I dare say you've found out. When I hear the birds all fluting away, I simply *ache* to join in."

"I didn't know grown-ups were like that," said Joyce with a startled glance at her.

"Oh, my *aunt*! Is *that* how I seem to you?"

"Well, you are, aren't you? If you had long hair it would be up, wouldn't it?" said Joyce in amazement.

Joey gripped hold of both pockets on her blazer. "My *dear* Joyce! How ever old do you think I am?"

"I hadn't thought about it. But the head-girl at the High was nearly nineteen, and *her* hair was up. And Marie and Frieda and Simone and Sophie and Bianca all have theirs up, and they're your chums."

"I'm not eighteen yet," interrupted Jo with great impressiveness. All the same, she looked grave. She was beginning to see that Gillian was right, and that she did seem rather inaccessible to the younger girls. "However, Joyce, my child, I'm going to talk to you like a Dutch uncle—or would 'aunt' be a better way of putting it? Look here, I know that Middles get full of beans at times; I did it myself when I was a Middle. But there are ways and ways of expressing it. Can't you find out some less essential way of doing it than you've tried lately?"

Joyce reddened. "I know I haven't always been as decent as I might."

"I'm saying nothing about that midnight feast of yours," went on Joey. "It never occurred to our crowd to want to do such a thing, which is rather queer when you come to think of it, for the girls here were always so awfully keen to 'be very English,' as they called it. They got hold of all sorts of school-stories, and tried to carry out as many of the ideas in them as they could." Here she stopped and grinned as she thought of some of those same stories.

"How did they do it?" asked Joyce curiously, forgetting that she had been on the point of resenting what promised to be a "pi-jaw."

"Well, the *Chaletian* arose out of that, for one thing. And another was the celebration of my sister's birthday. You know we always keep that as a holiday, even though she's been at the Sonn-alpe for three years now, don't you?"

Joyce nodded. "Corney told me about that—and that you all went to Oberammergau last year to see the Passion Play," she said.

"Well, those are two of the things. There were others—Oh, ask some of your own crowd to tell you if you must know!" said Jo; then added virtuously, "I am not going to give anyone away. But that's what I meant when I spoke of being full of beans. We weren't any of us archangels by any means. But we didn't count ragging a mistress in the particular way your crowd ragged Miss Norman as 'English fun.' It's too much like kicking someone weaker than yourself."

46

Joyce went beetroot colour. "I didn't think of it that way," she said ashamedly.

"I know. But look here, Joyce; supposing you had been in Miss Norman's place? She doesn't profess to teach elder girls, you know. The babies love her, and she's splendid with them. But she's taken on this extra job of helping you people with your languages so that you'll get on better in form. She does it in her own free time"—Jo, it is needless to state, knew nothing about the extra salary, and never even thought of it—"and then the only way you thank her is by behaving like little brutes—for you *were* brutal, you know!"

No one, so far, had put it to Joyce quite like this. She could go no redder, but her head drooped, and she felt more ashamed of herself than she had ever done in her life.

"You know," went on Joey conversationally, "I should never have thought that *you* would have gone in for that sort of thing. After all, it's hardly good enough, you know."

"I wasn't the only one," said Joyce after a long pause.

"No; but you were the chief one," retorted Joey. "I can guess it was your idea. You have brains, you know, even if you don't always use 'em!"

This silenced Joyce again. She had an idea that she ought to resent all this, but Jo's casual manner and that hint that she herself had never been a model disarmed her. Besides, she was still under the spell of Mademoiselle's last words to

47

her, and she was inwardly terrified lest the threat of expulsion should be carried out.

"Over this railing," said Jo as they reached the fence which divides Briesau from the lake-path to Geisalm, the next hamlet. "Keep up to the mountain-slope as far as you can. The rocks have been falling again, I see. If this goes on, we shan't be able to get along here in another year or two."

"What will you do then?" asked Joyce.

"No idea. I suppose they'll cut a path higher up, and bring it down further along to join the original one. This is always breaking away now. Bill says it's friable rock, but she thinks it doesn't go very far. She has an idea that probably this part was yards wider not so many years ago. However, I can't sure about it."

The two girls climbed the fence, and then for some distance hugged the mountain-side, for just here the path overhung the lake until it reached a wide fissure which was crossed by a plank bridge which ran a good distance into the path at either side.

"Know the story of this?" demanded Jo, waving her hand towards it. "We were here when it happened—Christmas term before last. *And* most of St Scholastika's. We'd got across, but some of the Saints, along with Miss Browne, hadn't. It was beginning to widen before that, and whether we set it going or not, I can't tell, but anyhow, it suddenly seemed to give, and there we were—planted there; for we couldn't possibly get back as it was. We had to go on to Geisalm, and then climb up the mountain to the big alm where a good many of the valley cattle are pastured in the summer, and where there is a little village called Mechtthau. Then we had to scramble down the other side, and so reach the Pass. It was winter, and the snow lay thick on the ground, and it had been freezing, so you can imagine what it was like. The Saints had only come that term, and weren't accustomed to climbing, and some of their Juniors were there, too. It was a nice little expedition, believe me! We were thankful to find haycarts waiting for us at the end of the Pass."

"But how did they know to come there?" asked Joyce, thankful that the conversation had left her own doings.

"Bill had rung up from Geisalm to the school to let them know; and, of course, the Fawn had to go back with the few left her, and she called in and told them. She was—well—rather agitated when it all happened," and Jo grinned puckishly at the remembrance.

"Why?" asked Joyce.

"My child, what a question! How d'you think you'd have felt if you'd been responsible for about thirty girls who were all at one side of a chasm while you were at the other? Especially when you'd *seen* the rocks avalanching down We daren't try to cross on the ice, either. There are springs all around here, and even in the hardest frosts it's not safe."

"Oh, I see.—Oh, Jo, is that the Dripping Rock?"

Jo nodded. "This is it. It's made by a tiny

stream that runs through the alm above and shoots over just here. She's spouting pretty well to-day," she added, with a glance at the water which was pouring over the edge of the shallow basin it had hollowed for itself in the huge rock that jutted out from the mountain wall. "We shouldn't be able to get to Geisalm to-day even if we wanted to, unless we were prepared to risk a wetting."

Joyce watched the hurrying water, enraptured. It crashed down on to the rock beneath, and then tore across it to fall into the lake. Jo let her stand for a few minutes, and then suggested that they had better turn. Otherwise they would be late for Kaffee und Kuchen.

"It's lovely," said Joyce with a final look as she turned and followed the head-girl along the path. "What is it like in winter when it's frozen? But perhaps it doesn't freeze?"

"Doesn't it just ! Oh, it's like a fairy-tale picture then, of course. And when the sun shines, and all the icicles sparkle, it's one of the loveliest sights I ever saw," said Jo. "Mind where you're going, Joyce. I don't like the look of the path. The rain we've had since Half-term seems to have loosened it a little."

"What would happen?" Joyce wanted to know.

"What happened before. It would vanish into the lake. And us with it !"

"Is the lake very deep here? Couldn't we swim somehow?"

"Oh, it's deep all right. This is one of the deepest parts. It varies very much, you know. But I shouldn't fancy a bath to-day. The springs keep it icy, even in summer, and what it must be like with all the ice and snow water from the mountains, I shiver to think. That's one reason why we never have swimming early."

However, they were not to be tested this time. They reached the fence in safety, and Jo vaulted over neatly, Joyce following her with a flying leap that made the head-girl open her eyes.

"I say! You're not a bad jumper!" she exclaimed. "Are you keen on gym?"

"Rather! If I'd got to earn my living, I'd like to be a gym mistress like Miss Nalder," said Joyce.

Jo glanced at her. "That means plenty of hard work, my child. For one thing, I know you've got to pass London Matric. to get into any decent college. You'll have to dig in at work if that's your idea."

"Oh, are you sure?" Joyce looked crestfallen. "I thought you'd only have to work at gym and folk-dancing."

"Oh, my goodness, no! There's heaps more than that to do," said Jo. "I know, because Grizel Cochrane, up at the Annexe, once thought of it, but her people wouldn't hear of it. You must do massage and anatomy, and lots like that. And you've got to be as strong as a horse, too."

"Well, I'm strong enough," said Joyce. "Bilious attacks are the only things that ever upset me." And then she suddenly went red as she remembered the cause of the last one.

"Then you'd better begin to pull up on your work," said Jo, kindly ignoring her blushes. She suddenly stood still and faced round on the younger girl. "Look here, Joyce; it's no business of mine, of course, but—*can't* you pull up a bit?" Then, as she saw the sulky resentment coming into Joyce's eyes, she added, "Think how bucked your mother would be! It would be as good as a tonic to her to hear you'd decided to pitch in and really do something. I don't believe you're stupid, you know," she went on. "You have got ideas, even if they aren't quite the right kind. If I were you, I'd produce some of the other, and show people what you've got in you. You *could*! Corney has, and if she has, then you can."

Joyce stood silent. Suddenly she looked up "Perhaps—Corney was a—much nicer girl than me all along," she said unevenly.

"Corney was a trial when she first came," said Jo lightly. "She'll tell you that much herself if you ask her." There was a pause. Then the head-girl suddenly touched the Middle lightly. "What about it, Joyce?"

Joyce laid her hand into the slender, tanned one Jo was offering her. "I'll—I'll have a shot," she promised.

"Good for you, I knew you'd be a sport if you tried," said Jo largely, and not altogether truthfully, for she had been doubtful on this point. "And now, my child, we must run, or we shall be late, and then there'll be a fuss!"

CHAPTER FOUR

THEKLA'S PLOT

WITH a resolution born of her promise to Joey, Joyce worked steadily during prep that evening. What is more, she really tried, a thing she had not once done since she entered the school. The result was that next day those of the Staff who dealt with the Lower Fifth were agreeably surprised by the quality of her work, and came to the conclusion that Mademoiselle's latest lecture must have done her all the good in the world.

Still better news came down from the Sonnalpe. Mrs Linton had passed an excellent night, and the doctors thought that if she continued to go on as she was doing, both the girls might spend the week-end with her. Joyce went to her dormitory that night feeling as if everything was going to go right. She had gained an A+ for her history, and B for both algebra and French. During prep, she again worked with all her might, refusing to heed anything else, and turning a cold shoulder to all Thekla's whispers. The rest of the form regarded her with curiosity, wondering what on earth had happened to her to change her so completely. Gillian, catching her sister for ten minutes before Abendessen, went off after that meal to dance in the common-room quite happily, for Joyce had whispered, "I'm going to try hard with my lessons, Gill—really I am! Do you think Mummy will be bucked?"

"I should think she'll be so bucked when she hears that she'll be out of bed in no time," said Gillian, "Oh, Joycey, I *am* glad, darling!"

Altogether, as Joyce rose from her knees at the bedside and climbed into bed, she felt a much happier girl than she had been for some time. Violet and Greta bade her good-night quite pleasantly, and she replied gaily, "Good-night, and pleasant dreams!" Cornelia, by virtue of her additional year, did not come upstairs for another hour.

Joyce was tired, and soon drowsed off to sleep. She was wakened from a very sound slumber by someone shaking and even pinching her. She sat up, and almost uttered an exclamation. But a hand was slipped over her mouth, and a well-known voice whispered, "Hush! You must not cry out. I wish to speak with you now. Come!"

Greatly wondering, and still drowsy and somewhat confused, Joyce tumbled out of bed and looked for her dressing-gown. As tidiness was not one of her virtues, she failed to find that garment—it happened to be under the bed where she had dropped it before getting in—and went out into the moonlit corridor in her pyjamas With her tossed golden curls, her sleepy blue eyes, and her bare feet, she looked very small and young, and the girl who had summoned her in calm defiance of all rules, looked very much taller and older.

"What d'you want, Thekla?" asked Joyce, yawning drowsily. "And whatever time is it?"

"That is no matter," said Thekla. "I wish to speak with you, Joyce. Come to that window, and we will sit behind the curtains."

Joyce always took a little time to waken completely, so now she followed the elder girl to the window, and they sat down on the window-seat. Thekla pulled the chintz curtains across them, so that they were hidden from view—though anyone desiring to investigate must have noticed the suspicious-looking bulges.

"What is it?" repeated Joyce impatiently. "Do hurry up, 'cos it's fearfully cold, and there's a ghastly draught here—and anyway, it's against the rules!"

"It is this," said Thekla, paying no heed to what the child said. "I wish that you shall not be friends with Jo Bettany, for I hate her, and she shall not be friends with you."

Joyce was awake now with a vengeance. "I say, have you gone balmy?" she demanded.

"Balmy," repeated Thekla, to whom the word was new.

"Yes—moonstruck—dotty—oh, *mad,* then! 'Cos I never heard such rot in my life before! What business is it of yours *who* I'm friendly with, I'd like to know? D'you mean to say that you've dragged me out here and are making me break rules just to say things lie this? You must be completely off!"

Thekla's cold grey eyes grew colder, and her face set in hard lines. "It is that you are *my* friend, and I do not wish that you should friends with that horrible girl be," she said. "Do you hear, Joyce? I am older than you, and have the right to guide you—"

"I can see myself letting you!" retorted Joyce with more vigour than caution.

"Hush!" said Thekla imperatively. "You will rouse the others, and then there will be trouble."

"Don't care if I do!" Joyce was thoroughly angry. She had been wakened out of a sweet sleep, and brought here on a chilly night to talk rubbish about Jo Bettany who had been so kind to her. And, if you please, Thekla coolly claimed the right to choose her friends for her! The spoilt darling of the Lintons had never been treated like this before, and had no idea of submitting to it—the less so, since Thekla was deliberately making her break a stringent rule.

"I can tell you this, Thekla von Stift," she said furiously, "I shall choose my friends to suit myself. The *only* person who has any right to interfere with me that way is Mummy, and *she* won't when it's a girl as jolly decent as Joey Bettany. If you were more like her, it would be better for you!"

Joyce was quite right to be indignant; but she chose a most unwise way of showing her indignation. To be told that she ought to be more like Jo made Thekla nearly choke with rage. She gripped Joyce's wrist so tightly that the younger girl nearly cried out with the pain.

"How dare you—how dare you!" hissed the Prussian venomously. "You think you will treat me like a glove that you throw away because he has holes in him. But I will teach you, Joyce Linton! Yes; and I will on that Schweinhund, Jo Bettany, revenged be!'"

"'Schweinhund' is swearing," said Joyce nastily. "I should have thought—"

"Anyone there?"

The voice gave the pair in the window-seat an unpleasant shock, for it was the last thing they had expected. But Joyce had left the dormitory door open, and her own furious tones had awakened Cornelia Flower, head of the dormitory by virtue of her fifteen years, and she had come out to see what was going on. Her sharp eyes at once noticed the queer distortion of the curtain folds, and she made straight for the window and pulled them aside.

"Joyce Linton—and Thekla von Stift!" she exclaimed in her usual bell-like tones. "What on earth are you doing here at this time?"

"Be quiet!" hissed Thekla furiously. "You will us into trouble bring!"

"Well, what are you doing here?" demanded Cornelia, dropping her voice a little. "Do you know that it's after one?" And she glanced at the watch she had forgotten to remove from her wrist when she went to bed. "Joyce, get back to your cubey at once. If anyone catches you here there'll be the father and mother of a row!"

Joyce needed no second telling. Besides, she had been frightened by Thekla's rage, and still felt shaky. She slipped past Cornela, and reached the dormitory door before Thekla could recover her senses sufficiently to snatch at her and hold her back. But just as the child reached the door, she was held up by Miss Wilson's amazed tones.

"*Girls!* What are you doing here at this time of night?"

Joyce had been afraid of Thekla, but she was no coward. She shot back and stood beside Cornelia, who looked rather taken aback. Miss Wilson advanced along the corridor till she came up to the trio, at whom she looked so coldly that even Thekla's rage was cooled down, and she shivered a little.

"What are you doing here?" she asked again.

Even in that moment, Cornelia's brain was saying, "Her hair's naturally curly! Anyhow, she hasn't any pins in it. What a whacking plait! And, I say, she looks quite young! I guess she isn't so old after all!" At the same time, she said in her very blandest tones, "I heard a noise and came out, Miss Wilson. Perhaps Joyce and Thekla did the same."

Miss Wilson looked at the three closely, and for the first time was struck by the pinched blue look in Joyce's face. The child was shivering now, what with her light attire and the fresh chill of the early spring night. The mistress stretched out a hand, and took one of hers.

"Joyce! You are frozen with the cold! Why did you come out without your dressing-gown, whatever noise you may have heard? Here; come to my room all of you!" And without more ado she whirled them off to the pretty little room where she switched on her electric radiator—

stoves in the dormitories and passages were out now that the spring had come—and made them sit down beside it. Then, noticing that Joyce was still shivering, she stripped a blanket off the bed, and rolled her in it before she ran down to the kitchen to purloin a jug of milk and three mugs. Then she came back, plugged in her milk-heater, and dropped it into the jug. While the milk was warming, she sat down, and turned to Cornelia again.

"Now, Cornelia, I want to know the meaning of all this.—Joyce, are you getting warm?"

"Yes, thank you, Miss Wilson," said Joyce, who looked warmer already.

"Bill" nodded, and then turned to the young American. "Well, Cornelia?"

"It's just what I said, Miss Wilson," said Cornelia earnestly. "I heard a noise in the corridor, so I got up and went to see what it was."

"I see. I suppose you know that your yelling woke me? I only wonder the whole house isn't raised! When do you mean to learn to moderate your tones, Cornelia?"

"I'm sorry," apologised Cornelia, the pink in her cheeks deepening.

"Well, it's all right as it happens.—Now, Thekla, you are next oldest in age—wait, though, aren't you older than Corney? Yes? I thought so. Now will you be so good as to tell me what took you into the corridor at one o'clock in the morning?"

"It—it is as Cornelia has said," said Thekla, carefully avoiding looking at either Cornelia or

Joyce. "I hear a noise in the passage and I go to see what makes him, and then I see Joyce. I was asking why she was there, and Cornelia came."

The other two girls were startled into silence. Cornelia, knowing where she had found the two, and how, was so taken aback at this flagrant falsehood, that she had nothing to say. As for Joyce, that lie of Thekla's ended the last feeling of friendship between them. She sat up, looking a little warmer for "Bill's" prompt treatment, and faced the mistress.

"I didn't hear any noise in the corridor, Miss Wilson. I—" Then she came to a sudden full stop. She could not tell the exact truth, for that would mean giving Thekla away, and whatever the Prussian might have done, Joyce was too well trained in the schoolgirl's code to tell tales. So she stopped short and went red.

Miss Wilson got up, and went to the table to test the milk. It was hot now, and she poured it out, and gave each of the girls a mugful. "Drink that, girls," she said briefly. "Now, Joyce, when you have finished, I want to know what woke you in the first instance."

Joyce drained her milk, and set the mug down, feeling considerably better for the hot drink. "I —a sound, Miss Wilson," she said in answer to the mistress's question.

"What sort of a sound?"

"A—a—whispery sort of sound, I think."

"Where was it—in the corridor? But you said you heard no sound in the corridor."

"I didn't."

"Where, then?"

Joyce set her lips and remained obstinately silent.

Miss Wilson glanced at her. Then the sound of the big clock striking two decided her to end the inquiry for the present. She turned to the other two: "Finished your milk? Then go back to bed at once, please. I will see you all in the morning. Joyce, as you have no slippers, and I am certain you would wake the whole house if you tried to flounder along in mine, I am going to carry you back. Come along!"

Joyce gasped; but Miss Wilson was already as good as her word, and had swung her up in strong, capable arms, and was carrying her, blanket and all, back to the dormitory. It was less exacting than it sounds, for Joyce was small and lightly built for her age, and Miss Wilson was tall and athletic, and made nothing of her light weight. She laid the child in her bed, still rolled up in the blanket, and tucked her in.

"You had better keep that round you for to-night, Joyce," she said. "You were very silly to go out without your slippers and dressing-gown, and I don't want you to start a cold, with the Sale of Work next week. Are you quite warm now? Let me feel your hands."

"Much warmer, thank you, Miss Wilson," murmured Joyce, who was on the verge of tears. She was worn out, and the unexpected kindness of the mistress she had always regarded as her pet abhorrence, had unnerved her. Perhaps Miss

Wilson realised this. She made sure that the froggy paws were warming up, tucked the bed-clothes more securely round the child, and then left her, and went to see that Cornelia was safe in bed. She finished by visiting Thekla, but that young lady was apparently asleep, so Miss Wilson, having closed the door behind her, retired to her own room, where she spread her travelling-rug on the bed to make up for the blanket wrapped round Joyce, and settled down to finish her own disturbed slumbers.

Next morning she sent word to the three that she would see them in the chemistry laboratory at Break; they were to come to her as soon as the bell sounded and bring their cocoa and biscuits with them. Joyce had tried to get hold of Thekla to ask her what she had meant by her extraordinary statements, but the elder girl kept out of her way; and as Joyce had extra German for the first period, and Thekla did not take algebra, it was comparatively easy for her to avoid the English child.

As for Cornelia, she had looked at Thekla once with such meaning in her eyes, that that young person had gone fiery red, and turned hastily away. Things were not going to be quite as easy as she had imagined, but she had decided on her story, and she meant to stick to it. Joyce should regret her temerity of the night before; and since Jo Bettany had obviously decided to take up the younger Linton, then Jo should be hurt by Joyce's hurt.

When Break came, Cornelia marched up to

Joyce. "Come along," she said. "Bill will be waiting for us, I expect."

"What have you been up to, Corney?" demanded Evadne, overhearing this.

"Tell you later," said Cornelia. "Bill told us to get our cocoa and biscuits and go to her at once, so we'd better."

"I guess you had," agreed her compatriot. "Bill don't like being kept waiting one mite, though she does make such a fuss about being patient and persevering."

The two got their cocoa and biscuits, and then went off, not waiting for Thekla, who had not yet come from the extra English lesson she had at this period. They went to the laboratory, where Miss Wilson was waiting for them, her cocoa before her. She was nibbling a biscuit thoughtfully, and when she saw them, waved them to one of the benches. "You had best sit down, girls," she said. "We must wait for Thekla, of course, so get on with your lunch while you wait."

Thekla came a few minutes later. There was a cold light in her eyes, and her lips were set in a straight line.

"You are late," said Miss Wilson coldly.

"Miss Annersley did not finish," said Thekla sulkily.

"I see. In that case I must excuse you. Sit down, and let us get this over.—First of all, Joyce, I wish to know why you were out on the corridor last night. You told me that you heard a noise, but it was not out there. Where was it, then?"

"In my cubicle," said Joyce, who had decided that she might say so much.

"In your cubicle? And pray, what made it?"

Joyce was silent. Thekla might tell as many lies as she chose, but Joyce was not going to give her away. The mistress, guessing partly at what lay behind her silence, left her, and turned to the German girl.

"I will hear your story while Joyce is deciding to obey me, Thekla," she said. "Why were you out there in the first instance? You can scarcely have heard any noise in Joyce's cubicle, as your own dormitory is at the other end of the passage."

"That is true," said Thekla, fixing her eyes on her cocoa. "But I heard Joyce walking in the corridor, and I went to see what was wrong. I feared that the house on fire might be."

"Nonsense!" said Miss Wilson sharply. "If that had been the case you would certainly have heard more than Joyce's footsteps. And as it is, I cannot imagine how you heard those, since she was barefoot."

"Still, I did hear them," said Thekla sulkily. "I heard the pit-pat, and went to see who it was and what was wrong. It might have been someone who was ill. I did not know."

Cornelia deliberately turned round, and looked at her. Then she set down her mug with decision. Thekla changed colour. She was only sixteen, and though she could tell lies quite brazenly, there was something in the other girl's action that upset her. Miss Wilson took no notice of the American's action, but went on with her catechism. "Well; so you heard a noise and went to investigate. Go on!"

"I found Joyce in the corridor," went on Thekla, still not looking at anyone. "I went to ask her what she did there, for it is against the rules. Then Cornelia did come out, and you also, and that is all."

Miss Wilson was silent for a moment. "Who is the head of your dormitory?" she asked at length.

"It is Margia Stevens," said Thekla, lifting her eyes in amazement.

"Cornelia, go and bring Margia here, please."

Cornelia got up and went off. As she went, she gave Thekla another of those straight, hard stares, and again Thekla went red.

"Finish your biscuits while you are waiting," said Miss Wilson briefly; and she drank the last of her own cocoa.

Margia, looking rather guilty—she was racking her brains for the reason for this summons, and could find none, having a fairly clear conscience for once—entered the room a minute or two later with Cornelia behind her, and came to attention before the mistress.

"Did you hear any noise last night after you had gone to bed, Margia?" asked "Bill," plunging headlong into things.

"Yes, Miss Wilson," said Margia. "I heard the dormitory door open and Thekla come in. I knew it was Thekla from the cubey she went to. Then I heard you follow, and, of course, there were voices in the corridor. But as I knew you were there, I thought I had better not interfere."

"I see. Nothing else?"

"No, Miss Wilson."

"Thank you. You may go—Oh, wait a moment! Are you sleeping better now?"

Margia, who had been suffering from slight insomnia lately, nodded. "Yes; much better, thank you."

"Still wake easily, I suppose?"

"Fairly easily, Miss Wilson."

"And do you find it an easy matter to see that your dormitory get up when the rising-bell goes?"

"Yes, thank you. As a rule it is quite easy."

"Who are the most difficult to rouse?"

With her eyes wide with wonder, Margia replied, "Thekla and Hilda are the worst, Miss Wilson. I had to shake Thekla this morning," she added.

"Thank you. Then that is all. Please do not repeat what I have said."

"No, Miss Wilson." And Margia withdrew, nearly ill with curiosity.

When she had gone, Miss Wilson turned to Thekla again. "Well, Thekla?"

Thekla sat in sullen silence.

"What have you to say?"—and oh! the cutting ring in Miss Wilson's usually pleasant tones! —"You claim to have heard a noise that did not disturb a girl who is a notoriously light sleeper, while you, who are evidently a heavy one, were awakened by it. Margia's cubicle is near the door; yours, as I noticed last night, is at the other end of the room. I should like to know the meaning of all this."

"I—I was awake before," stammered Thekla, rather losing her head.

"Indeed? You gave me to understand that it was the noise of Joyce's footsteps that roused you."

There was a really ghastly pause after this. The bell rang for the end of Break, but Miss Wilson took no notice of it, so the girls were unable to do so. It was a free period for the mistress, and she simply carried on with her interrogation, regardless of what her compeers might have to say over the absence of the three from their classes.

"Once more, Joyce," said Miss Wilson, turning to the youngest of the trio, "I ask you what it was that disturbed you? You may as well tell me," she added, "for I intend to know, and you all stay here till I do. Also, though the code of never telling tales is, as a rule, quite justifiable, I am afraid you must break it for once. I cannot imagine that any girl in your circumstances would be likely to do such a mad thing as to break a rule about leaving your dormitory after Lights Out without an adequate excuse. Besides, the very fact that you were merely in your pyjamas and had not even troubled to put on your bedroom slippers points to the fact that you were roused out of your sleep suddenly. Who roused you—Thekla?"

Joyce literally jumped, for Miss Wilson shot out the last word at her with the suddenness of a boomerang. Also, she was startled by the perspicuity of the mistress.

"Answer me, Joyce!"

"I—I—" stammered poor Joyce in a regular quandary.

"Miss Wilson, I'll bet my bottom dollar it *was* Thekla!" burst out Cornelia at this point. She had been aching to speak, but respect for Miss Wilson had kept her silent up till now. "Joyce won't tell you, but I am going to *report* as head of her dormitory that when I heard the sound of voices in the corridor and went out, I saw a queer bulge in the curtains over the window where we were when you came. I pulled them apart, and Joyce and Thekla were both there, sitting in the window-seat; Thekla had hold of Joyce, and Joyce looked scared out of her seven senses. Maybe I've no right to go horning in like this, but I guess I'm not leaving this story to a girl who's told you nothing but dead-straight *lies* about it all!"

"Thank you, Cornelia; that will do," said Miss Wilson, recovering her self-possession, of which Cornelia's sudden descent into the arena had robbed her. "Kindly refrain from using slang, and leave Joyce to answer for herself."

But if her words were tart, her tone was not, and Cornelia suppressed a grin with difficulty.

"Now, Joyce," said the mistress, turning to the

child once more, "I am still waiting for an answer to my question."

Seeing that Cornelia had already given away things most handsomely, Joyce looked up, very flushed and uncomfortable. "Corney is right, Miss Wilson. But I'd never have told you if she hadn't got it first shot," she said.

"So I gather," replied Miss Wilson drily. "I wish you people would try to realise that there are times and seasons when the schoolgirl code cannot be followed implicitly. I should like the full story, please.——Cornelia, I do not think you can help us any further, and you have only missed a quarter of an hour of your lesson, so perhaps you had better go to your form-room and make the most of what is left. Who is with you now?"

"Mademoiselle Lachenais for French translation," said Cornelia, whose face had fallen appreciably at this.

"Please give my apologies to Mademoiselle Lachenais, and tell her I will see her about Joyce and Thekla at the end of the morning," said Miss Wilson, "and explain why I have detained you also."

"Yes, Miss Wilson."

Cornelia left the room quietly, but once the door was safely shut behind her, she paused to execute a dance of rage at being sent away just when things promised to become really interesting. As Mademoiselle Lepâttre happened to be coming along in search of Miss Wilson, she got the full benefit of it, and Cornelia received a

sharp reprimand for her behaviour, which, however, did not subdue her noticeably. Then she
was dismissed to her form-room, and had to go
with becoming sedateness, while Mademoiselle
opened the laboratory door, and walked in on a
scene she had little anticipated.

"And now, Thekla," Miss Wilson was saying,
"I should like your account of last night's per-
formance once more; and please tell me the truth
this time."

It was at this point that Mademoiselle, still
somewhat annoyed at Cornelia's outrageous behaviour, irrupted into the room and into the very
middle of things. Naturally Miss Wilson had to
give some explanation, and she told the whole
in a few bald words.

Mademoiselle looked anxiously at Joyce.
"Joyce, is this the truth, my child?"

"Yes, Mademoiselle," replied Joyce.

"What have you to say, Thekla?"

Thekla shrugged her shoulders. Her plot to get
Joyce into trouble with Mademoiselle, and so
hurt Jo Bettany who had taken her up, had gone
wrong, thanks to Cornelia Flower. Well, she
must just acknowledge it, and plan better another time.

"As you know all now, it is of little use my
saying anything," she said in her own language.

"Joyce, you may go," said Mademoiselle
gently. "Miss Wilson will finish with you later
on. Please explain to the mistress in charge of
your form."

She looked at "Bill" as she spoke, and that

lady nodded. Joyce departed, rather inclined to wonder if she were standing on her head or her heels. As Mademoiselle Lachenais, good-natured as she was as a rule, was annoyed at the way her class was being broken up, she was received with the terse remark, "You may go to your seat. We will continue with this matter of your lateness after the lesson!"

Joyce sat down, and ten minutes afterwards proceeded to make a thorough mess of the paragraph she had to translate. However, when Mademoiselle Lachenais understood it all, she forgave the child, and remitted the detention and bad mark she had awarded.

Meanwhile, Mademoiselle Lepâttre was busy with Thekla.

"Will you please bring Thekla to the study, Miss Wilson?" she had said, and, shepherded by the science mistress, Thekla duly went to the study, prepared to receive another severe lecture. It never came. Mademoiselle catechised her closely until she had got the whole story. Then she leaned back in her chair and looked across at Miss Wilson.

"Will you please take Thekla von Stift to Matron?" she said, a cold incisiveness in her tones. "Then I should be glad if you would ask Miss Annersley, Miss Stewart, and Mademoiselle Lachenais to join us here. They may set their forms work to do, and perhaps you would ask Josephine Bettany to send prefects to sit with any forms thus left who are below Upper Fifth."

Miss Wilson got up. "Certainly, Mademoiselle," she said.

She took Thekla, now becoming vaguely uneasy, out of the room, and handed her over to Matron. Then she sought out the three members of Staff Mademoiselle had named, and returned with them to the study. For an hour the five mistresses were closeted together, but at the end of that time they had come to a final decision. A message was sent to Matron, who brought her prisoner down to the study once more. Mademoiselle put two questions—and two only—to Thekla. The venom in the replies settled the matter.

"I did it because I hate Jo Bettany, and Joyce was becoming friendly with her," declared the Prussian girl. "I knew that if Joyce got into bad trouble, it would grieve Jo—if Joyce were expelled, then Jo would be hurt; so as Joyce would not give up this so-foolish new friendship of hers, I decided to do it to punish them both. No; I am not sorry I did it. At least it will have given Joyce a nasty fright."

"Do you realise what you are saying, Thekla?" demanded Miss Annersley, who was the first to recover her breath after this.

Thekla's eyes glinted. "Yes; I know. But I tell you, I hate Jo; and now I hate Joyce too. I meant to harm them—I am only sorry I did not succeed. For I suppose Joyce will be forgiven, since you have found it all out."

The mistresses looked at each other. It was plain that in her present mood Thekla would listen to nothing. There was only one thing to do.

"I am sorry, Thekla," said Mademoiselle slowly, still speaking in the German which had been used throughout the interview. "We have done our best for you. Had you expressed sorrow for your wrong-doing, it might have been just possible to give you another chance. But your only sorrow is because your wicked plans have not succeeded. Our best has done you no good. For the first time in the history of the School we have to say that a girl is gaining no good here. Instead, you are doing actual harm. That cannot be permitted, so we must send you away."

"Send me away?" Thekla did not understand.

"Yes; expel you, as you would have got Joyce expelled if you had had your own way. You have proved yourself to be ruthless, vindictive, and unchristian. We cannot keep you here. I will telegraph to your father now—this very afternoon, asking him to come and take you away Until he does so, you will remain in the Sanatorium, for I cannot allow you to associate with the other girls. You will never be left alone, for we are unable to trust you—you have no sense of honour. Now you will go with Matron, and your possessions will be brought to you from your dormitory.—Take her away, please, Matron. I will send someone to relieve you of your watch presently."

Thekla went white to the lips. She had never expected this to happen, and her pride was bitterly hurt. It had seemed to her that *she* had bestowed an honour on the School by coming to it. Now, it seemed that the School did not want her. More; she was told that she was a harm to the School.

"You cannot do this," she said slowly. "For just that one little fault you cannot do this thing."

"Ah, if it were only a *little* fault—or only *one* thing!" said Mademoiselle sadly. "But it is an accumulation of things, Thekla, all ending in this big thing. No; you need plead no more, for I shall not listen to you. I cannot do it. The Being to Whom you must now go is God, Whom you have hurt by your wickedness far more than even Joyce or Josephine. You are untrustworthy and deceitful. Last term you showed us that you were bad-tempered and selfish. At the beginning of this term you proved yourself greedy, and you end with this wicked plan of revenge against a girl who had not harmed you at all. What is worse, to make for the success of your plan you thought to use a girl who is two years younger than you and whom you had called your friend. If you had succeeded, it would in all probability have meant the death of Mrs Linton. I want you to think of that, Thekla—to remember that it is only by God's mercy that you are not, indirectly, at least, a murderess."

"That is not true! You are cruel to say such things to me!" Thekla was broken at last. Something in Mademoiselle's solemn tones struck home, and wakened her conscience at long last.

74

"No, Thekla; I am not cruel. I should be so if I allowed you to leave us without doing one final thing to try to bring you to a knowledge of how far along the road to wickedness you have gone. I pray God that this terrible knowledge may prove to be your help and safeguard for the future against such things. Now go with Matron. When I have heard from your parents, I will see you again."

Sobbing, all her hard, silly pride gone, Thekla stumbled out of the room. Never before had her conduct been put before her in such plain language, and she shrank back appalled from the ugly picture she saw.

The girls never saw her again, for her father came to take her away two days later, and in his silent fury at the account the School had to give of her, Thekla read his opinion of her conduct, and it added to her suffering. She expressed no sorrow for what she had done, then. But years later, when Mademoiselle had almost forgotten her own words to the girl, a letter came from her, acknowledging that she had deserved all that had been said to her, and telling how it had indeed been a safeguard to her. She begged the pardon of all concerned, and hoped they would send her their forgiveness.

CHAPTER FIVE

THE SUPPRESSION OF "BILL"

"It is my wish," said Mademoiselle, "that the matter should not be discussed. Thekla has gone. She is the first—the only—girl with whom we have failed. That is not pleasant to remember. So, girls, if you should hear any of the younger ones speaking of it, please hush them. We will try to forget as soon as possible."

"Yes, Mademoiselle," murmured the prefects en bloc.

"That is all, then. Now will you bring out the boxes and let me see what we have for the Sale."

Thankful to have heard the last of Thekla and her doings, the nine jumped to their feet and made for the big cupboard, where, carefully stored in boxes and cases, were the many things they had collected for their annual Sale of Work. The proceeds of the Sale always went to the free ward in the Sanatorium, the Chalet School providing one bed, the Annexe having undertaken another, and the Saints (as they called the girls of St Scholastika's, the school the other side of the lake) being responsible for a third. The Guides and Brownies of both schools supported a fourth between them, but they usually did it out of their funds, and an entertainment which they gave during any term that seemed suitable.

This year they had all resolved to make the Sale as big as possible, and although nothing has been said about it so far, they had given up as much of their free time as possible towards making various articles for it. Mademoiselle fingered sets of delicately embroidered collars and cuffs, and many others made in pillow-lace—for a goodly number of the Seniors were keen on this work, and some of them were very clever at it. There were also long strips of lace, and handkerchiefs edged with it. Then she had to look through a small hill of fancy-work of all kinds. Marie von Eschenau had taken up painting on china, in imitation of her sister, Wanda, and she had some very charming results to show. Wanda herself had sent her usual contribution of the same sort of thing, and as the Juniors had been doing pottery for handwork that term, there was quite an appreciable amount of crockery. Joey's hobby was cutting jig-saw puzzles, and she had cut thirty of all sizes. The Staff had undertaken to provide a sweets and confectionery stall, and were all hard at work in the Domestic Economy kitchen, turning out cakes and bonbons of all sorts. Matron had donated twenty dozen pots of home-made jam, which always found a ready sale. Even the domestic staff had contributed sundry pieces of embroidery and wood-carving.

"Mademoiselle," said Jo solemnly, "as we have all this china this year, can't we have a kind of bric-à-brac stall, with it and the wood-carvings and Simone's leather-work and my puzzles?"

"Shall we have enough?" asked Mademoiselle cautiously.

"Yes; I think so. There is still some more to come in, and Grizel promised some of that Florentine leather-painting she's been doing lately. It hasn't arrived yet—I expect she'll bring it down when she comes with the children. But with all that, I think we certainly *could* manage a stall."

"Well, let me see," mused Mademoiselle. "We shall have one fancy-work stall; one of plain needlework—these baby-clothes are beautiful, Bianca—one for sweets and cakes and jam; and this one that you suggest—besides the one for the Annexe, and the one for St Scholastika's. There are those water-colour sketches from the art classes, Jo. We might add those to your bric-à-brac stall. And the Juniors will have their lucky dip as usual. How are you going to arrange it this year?"

"Well, we thought of a Wishing Well," said Jo. "We've got that well in the acting-cupboard. If we set it on one of the mistresses' platforms, then two of the children could stand below and put the prizes into the bucket. We could arrange the platform as a kind of mossy bank with art muslin and creeper-plants, and it would look very pretty."

"I have a still better idea, my Jo!" interrupted Simone excitedly. "We have the dress for the Frog Prince. Let one of them wear that, and be the Frog to put the gifts into the bucket. And deck another as the Princess."

Jo solemnly stretched across the table and felt her head. "Quite cool!" she remarked. "It's a stroke of genius, Simone, and that's a strain on the best brain, so don't have another for some time to come, or we shall have you down with brain-fever."

"I wish you would not ruffle my hair," protested Simone, whose hair was just long enough to turn up in a roll at the base of her head, and who found it none too easy to keep it tidy as yet.

"Que vous êtes bébé!" said Mademoiselle with a shake of her head at Jo. "Simone, my child, your hair is hanging loose at the right side. Pray go and coiffe again, I beg you."

"I have to spend so much time that way," sighed Simone, leaving the room to obey orders.

Her cousin—Mademoiselle was a half-cousin of Simone's—laughed and turned to the business in hand. "Well, we will have the stalls, then, and the Wishing-Well as you suggest. St Scholastika's will also have a stall, and they will use the conservatory and make there a Magic Cave, for so Miss Browne told me over the telephone this morning. Then the Annexe will have their stall also, and that will be sufficient. And for entertainments—"

"Variety show in the common-room," said Jo briskly. "Clock-golf—and I hope to goodness Elsie and Evvy can explain it lucidly to those who don't know it!—if fine, in the garden. Folk-dance display in the Third—good thing it's a large room—and tea and refreshments in the Speisesaal. Frau Mieders is taking charge of that, and the two Matrons are helping her with some of the babes—I forget which, but they know. Miss Wilson and Miss Stewart are being responsible for the show, and Miss Nalder will see to the dancing. Then Herr Laubach is going to have the Fifth for his lightning sketches, and the St Scholastika competitions will be held in the Lower Fifth, with two of their staff in charge. Who is going to be responsible for the Bishop?"

"I will, naturally," replied Mademoiselle. "And Frieda must be there, too, for he is her uncle."

"I only hope he likes his fountain-pen," sighed Jo. "If he'd been a woman we'd have got the usual bouquet and no worry. But you can't offer a man—least of all a *bishop*—a bunch of flowers. —You're sure it's a fine nib he likes, Frieda?"

Frieda nodded. "Oh, yes; I asked him," she said calmly.

"You *asked* him? Do you mean he knows what to expect?"

"Oh, no! But I said I liked his fine, clear writing, and how did he do it," she explained. "When he wrote back, he thanked me for the compliment, and said it was because he always used a very fine pen."

"Well, the one we've got is a regular needle-point, so it *ought* to be all right", said Jo. "That was a real brain-wave, Frieda."

"Well, I think we have now settled all," said Mademoiselle. "I rang up St Scholastika's before I came up, and Miss Browne informs me that they will be here at half-past fourteen to help prepare everything. There is now half an hour left before Mittagessen, so I suggest that you should go out and play on the field till the bell rings."

They were very willing to go, and got up an impromptu hockey-practice for the short time. After Mittagessen, they rested for the prescribed half-hour, and then the sound of voices and the tramp of many feet outside told them that the Saints were arriving, and Joey fled to the door to bid them welcome.

They were led by Gipsy Carson, the head-girl and a great friend of Jo's, and Hilda Wilmot, a dreamy, artistic girl. Other members of the Chalet School greeted the newcomers joyously, for during the eighteen months that St Scholastika's had been established on the Tiernsee, the girls had fraternised a good deal, though at the beginning there had been a feud which nearly caused a tragedy at the two schools. However, that, as Mr Kipling says, is another story, and has been told elsewhere. Now, the two communities were great friends, and shared the visiting staff at the Chalet among them. The Chalet was the larger school, for St Scholastika's was for English girls only. But there was room for both, and both were prospering finely.

"Hello, Gyp!" called Jo to her friend. "You're in good time."

"I know we are," said Gipsy, as she followed the head-girl of the Chalet to the cloakroom to discard her hat and coat and change her shoes. "The Fawn thought we'd better get off as there's a good deal to do. And then Anders was getting fussed about the competitions. The Fourth are to have charge of those under her and Soamesy, you know, and they need a lot of arranging, I believe."

"Well, we'll need all our time," said Jo. "Come along, and let's get going."

Accompanied by Hilda and two other girls, Elspeth Macdonald and Maisie Gomm, they made for the big hall where the stalls were to be erected, while the others followed them, bearing baskets, boxes, and parcels, containing all the articles they had made or begged for the Sale.

"Where are we?" asked Gipsy.

"Over here between these windows. There are your frames—Eigen and Andreas were down this morning and set them up while were were at lessons. Your art muslin and other props arrived just before Mittagessen, and are behind. If you want tacks or drawing-pins or anything like that, you must go to Mademoiselle Lachenais at that table. She's got charge of them."

"Right!" said Gipsy. "I say; these are jolly decent frames!"

"They are—and pretty strong, too. Well, can you manage? I ought to be getting on with the bric-à-brac stall over there."

"With the *what* stall?"

"Bric-à-brac. Don't they teach you French at St Scholastika's?" demanded Jo, cheerfully insulting.

"They do. To my sorrow I know it. On the whole, I think I'll send Hilda over to Maddy to ask for nails and things. I see she's chumming with Mademoiselle Lachenais as usual, and I'd rather not remind her that I exist just at present."

Jo raised her eyebrows in a question, but Gipsy merely shook her head and looked provoking, so the head-girl of the Chalet left her friend to her own devices, and went across to the big frame which had somehow to be turned into the cottage of the Seven Dwarfs.

Joyce, who was standing there with her arms full of canvas painted to imitate a tiled roof, heaved a sigh of relief. "Oh, Jo! Thank goodness! What am I to do with all this?"

"Oh, shove it down somewhere, and then go and ask for two boxes of tacks and three hammers," said Jo easily. "Who else is supposed to be helping here?"

"Gill and Corney, and—oh, most of our crowd," said Joyce easily. "Lonny and Cyrilla are coming along with the ivy-trails and those long sprays of artificial wild-roses from the acting-cupboard."

Jo whistled. "I say! You are an energetic crowd! What are the rest going to do?"

"Well, Marie is turning the fancy-work stall into the Garden of the Beast in 'Beauty and the Beast,'" said Joyce as she piled her load behind the stall. "She's begged all the pot-plants she can get, and all those tree-flats you have for gloomy woods and so on for the stage. Frieda is busy with the Wishing-Well, and Simone and Bianca are doing plain-work into the Sleeping Beauty, though how they are going to get anyone to *sleep* all the afternoon and evening is more than I know!" she finished with a giggle, and Jo chuckled too.

"Well, go and get the nails and things," she said when she was grave again. "*I* will mount up yonder, and begin to fit those roof-things on."

She suited the action to the word, and climbed up on to the stall. Then she called loudly to Luise Rotheim who was standing near to hand her up one of the "roofs," and work began.

The big room rang with the noise of hammering, and there were frequent bursts of laughter, punctuated by shrieks as someone hammered a finger rather than a nail. Sophie Hamel had undertaken to help with the Annexe stall, and was surrounded by a bevy of small girls, all very eager to help, and most of them hindering as she tried to turn the bare wooden frame into something that would give some idea of Rapunzel's tower. It was no easy matter, and, as she said, how people could be expected to take an interest in a tall white thing was beyond her to fathom.

"It looks exactly like a tall candle," said Jo, passing it during the afternoon.

"I know," confessed Sophie. "But what can I do? It won't look so bad when we get Rapunzel's hair floating down it, perhaps."

"Who on earth is to be Rapunzel?" demanded Anne Seymour, pausing on her way to the Speisesaal with a trayful of vases.

"No one. We are to use a model my father has lent us."

"Good thing, too," said Jo.

"Yes; you could not expect any of the Annexe to sit up there all the afternoon," agreed Marie von Echenau, who had left her own labours on the Garden of the Beast, and come across to see how Sophie was progressing.

"But how do you make the hair?" asked Bianca from the next stall.

"It is skeins of golden knitting-silk all plaited together," said Sophie. "My father used it for part of his Christmas decorations, in one of his shop-windows, and he sent it up to us when I told him about this. The articles for sale are to be fastened to the silk. And that also is his idea."

"He's got jolly good ones," said Jo. "No wonder he's got such a top-hole place in Innsbruck!" Then she ambled back to her own stall, which was beginning to look more like a cottage now that the "roofs" were firmly fixed.

"Shall I put up the sides now, Jo?" asked Joyce eagerly. "Doesn't it look rip—er—jolly?"

"Very," said Jo amiably, passing over her slip. "Yes; I should think you might."

Joyce went flying to the corner where stood the "flats" with white cotton tacked lightly across them to represent white-washed walls, and came presently, breathlessly lugging one, for they were an awkward shape to manipulate in the crowded room. Jo helped her to fix it firmly across the front, hiding the skeleton framework, and then turned to see that the other two were put in place. They were firmly lashed, for no one wanted any trouble with them falling down during the Sale itself, and then the trickiest part of the work began.

Joey had set her heart on decorating her "cottage" so that it looked as if it were covered with ivy and roses. The men who worked for the school had been busy all the day before, getting trails of ivy and other climbing plants, and there were plenty for everyone.

"You people choose out the longest trails and hand them up to Eva and me," said Jo. "We'll stand on the counter part and fasten them up Then you can secure them at the bottom. Only do leave spaces so that people can see what we've got."

"We might interlace them across," suggested Eva, a quiet, steady girl, who, without being very noticeable, was yet a quiet influence for good in the School.

"Good idea! Hand me that hammer, Gill, and *don't* forget what I said about leaving spaces to show our goods."

Jo and Eva mounted on the stalls, for the three step-ladders had already been grabbed by other people; indeed the tallest of them, set on the stall itself, formed the framework for Sophie's "tower."

"This will be rather difficult," remarked Eva as she manœuvred to a position where she could get the trails fixed beneath the "roof." "Are we to put some over the roof too?"

"Oh, yes!" cried Joyce. "That will make it all the prettier. And sometimes the creepers go right across the roofs, you know.—Remember that cottage we had near Worthing, Gill? It had ivy all round the chimneys."

"*We* ought to have chimneys," said Jo. "Idiot that I was not to think of them!"

"But we can add them even now, can we not?" asked Eva, whose English was apt to be very formal.

"Yes; I suppose so. Here, Evvy—and you, Lonny! Hop up to the acting-cupboard and see if you can find any. There ought to be some there. We'll bag the steps when Marie has done with them, and stick them on after we've finished with this. Leave some sprays to twine round them, you people.—That's a good idea, Joyce; I'm glad you thought of it."

Evadne and Ilonka ran off to the big cupboard that ran all along one side of the top corridor, where all the acting properties were kept, and the rest set to work to arrange their decorations.

By Eva's advice, "windows" were made on a level with the counter of the stall, and they contrived to arrange their sprays so that these were left unveiled. Ivy formed the groundwork, and then Jo and Eva, working very carefully, fastened sprays of the artificial briar roses up one side, so as to give the effect of climbing roses.

"Oh, it looks simply gorgeous!" cried Joyce as she knelt beneath the erection, tying down some long sprays with which they had adorned the lower part. "It's just like a real cottage, isn't it, Hilda?"

Shy Hilda Bhaer nodded. "I think it is very

pretty," she said. "But it will be more like a cottage when it has its chimneys."

"Yes; what on earth are Lonny and Evvy doing?" asked Jo, pausing, hammer in hand, to look down the room to the door. "They must be *making* them, the time they are taking!"

"Oh, well, it gives us all the more time to finish this part of it," said Eva soothingly.

Crash! Yell! Simone had let her hammer fall dangerously near Mademoiselle Lachenais who was wandering round, admiring all the effects, and who had come within an ace of being brained by her young compatriot.

"Simone!" she cried when she had recovered from the shock. "Is it that you wish to slay me?"

"Oh, I beg your pardon, Mademoiselle," exclaimed the scarlet-faced Simone, descending from her ladder with more haste than grace. "I hope you are not hurt?"

"Simone, you really must be more careful!" said Miss Wilson, who had entered the hall in time to see this little episode, and had hastened up to make sure that no real harm had been done. "You might have hurt someone badly."

"Oh, I was not harmed," said good-natured little Mademoiselle Lachenais. "The hammer did not touch me."

"All the same, we don't want any accidents of that kind."

Simone, still scarlet, retrieved her hammer, and mounted once more to finish securing the cardboard outline of a spinning-wheel which surmounted their stall. The mistresses passed on to praise the Wishing-Well, and then stopped to admire the huge "tower" of Sophie, with Rapunzel already safely settled at the window.

"Are you sure it is quite safe, Sophie?" called up Mademoiselle with a laugh. "This so-tall tower of yours would do much harm if it should fall."

"I have blocked—no—*chocked*—the ladder with very big and heavy books, Mademoiselle," replied Sophie, who was standing at the top of the ladder, peering round the shop-window model her father had sent up the previous day. "Eigen has also lashed the ladder to the counter and the top bar of the stall, so I think it is quite safe. And we do not fasten the hair except just here among her own wig." And she waved the great plaits of golden-hued knitting-silk which she was preparing to attach to the model's own very yellow locks.

"This will be very effective," observed Miss Annersley, joining the other two mistresses at the foot of the erection.—"Well, my Robin, are you pleased with your stall?"

"But *yes*! I think it is *lovely*!" said the Robin with emphasis.

"And who is to be the Prince to stand at the foot of the hair?" asked Miss Wilson with a smile.

"Robin is," said Amy Stevens, sister of Margia of the Upper Fifth. "And *I'm* to be the old witch! Oo-ooh! Won't it be fun?"

The mistresses assented and went on, coming to

Jo's "cottage" just as the tardy messengers sent for the chimneys arrived, very dusty and untidy, for Evadne had torn her stocking, and Ilonka's long plait had come undone, and the heavy brown hair spread over her shoulders like a cloak.

"If length were all that was wanted, a good many of our girls might have acted Rapunzel very nicely," remarked Miss Wilson as they paused to watch the fun. "Frieda and Marie both have long fair hair, and now that Frieda has hers up, she is letting it grow properly. I saw it loose the other night, and fairly gasped at the quantity she has. It comes down to her hips."

"Oh, well, most Tyroleans seem to have long hair and plenty of it," said Miss Annersley. "They had to keep it shorter while it was down. You couldn't have hair like that falling into your work, my dear."

"No; I suppose not," acknowledged Miss Wilson.

"And why you should complain, I cannot think," added Mademoiselle Lachenais in her own language. "Your own hair comes below your waist."

"To my sorrow I know it. I'm often tempted to crop it. Only I think of the sensation it would create if I appeared in school with a shingle, and refrain from doing it," replied Miss Wilson. "Now what are those children going to do with those things?" And she turned an interested look at the "chimneys."

"I hope you've been long enough!" Jo was sarcastically greeting her messengers. "And what on earth have you done to yourselves? It's a good thing you get your hair washed to-night, Lonny, for 'dusty' simply doesn't describe its appearance!"

"I know. But the chimneys were behind everything else, and the things *are* dusty," said Ilonka, shaking back the heavy mane from her eyes "How are you going to get them up there, Jo?"

"I'll manage," said Jo confidently. "Gill, be a lamb and ask Marie if she's finished with the steps. If she hasn't, try Simone."

Gillian nodded, and went off to come staggering back with the steps. Cornelia, who had just finished fixing the last spray at the bottom, got up, stretched herself, and went to help her.

"They are Simone's!" gasped Gillian, who was hot and perspiring as a result of her journey "Oh, they are horrid things to carry! And people are so *rude*!"

"H'm! How many things have you knocked down?" asked Jo, descending to the floor as she spoke.—"Oh, sorry, Lonny! Was that your foot?"

"No; but it is not your fault that it was not!" retorted Ilonka, who had let out a strangled yelp as Jo dropped very nearly on top of her. "You will injure someone before the day is ended, Jo; I am certain of it!"

"Certain your granny!" was Jo's response to this.

"*Not* very witty," said Miss Wilson, coming up. Since when have *you* descended to the use of Third Form repartee, Jo?"

Jo jumped. She had not seen the mistresses before this. She also went very red, and Miss Wilson, in mercy, moved away.

"Let's get these chimneys up," said Gillian, coming to the rescue of what looked like developing into an awkward pause. "How d'you propose to set about it, Joey?"

"Climb the ladder, which we'll set at the side there, and slide them on," said Jo, recovering herself again. "Get them set up properly, you two. You know how to fasten them, don't you?"

They did. The chimneys were set up four-square, and then secured by means of clips which would be turned to the back so that the visitors would not see them. They were made with triangular openings at two opposite sides, and could be slid along the ridge-pole of the "roof" into place. Then someone would have to be stationed inside to fasten the under-clips to hold them steady.

"You'd better go under, Eva, and fasten them," said Jo.

But at that moment there was a call for Eva elsewhere, so Gillian, as the next tallest, was shown what to do, and then sent inside, to climb up on the counter in readiness for the coming of the chimneys.

Evadne and Ilonka finished setting them up, and then Evadne went off in response to a summons from Elsie to come and see about the clock-golf, and two of the others hastily pulled the ladder into position, without very much heed as to whether it was properly set out or not. Jo climbed up it, Cornelia mounting up to the cross-bar on the other side to steady the erection as she took the first. The chimneys *were* heavy things to manage, as the girls had said; and now they were set up, they were exceedingly awkward. Jo found that she must climb to the top step before she could set on the one she had. She had expected to be able to manage by stretching up, but she was unable to steady the weight. As it was, Cornelia had to make a long leg to the second cross-bar and stand there ready to help her.

The Staff had moved on before this; but just at this moment Miss Wilson heard her name uttered in plaintive tones by Simone, and turned back to go to her. She reached the cottage of the Seven Dwarfs just as Jo, with a final effort, got the chimney fitted down on the roof. Cornelia, her own part over, jumped down to be ready with ivy-sprays to twine round it. Whether she shook the ladder or not with her jump, it is hard to say.—Cornelia was fairly solid, and she jumped clumsily for once. Gillian always declared that at that identical moment Jo overbalanced herself. However it happened, the fact remains that Jo, standing on the topmost step, gave a sudden lurch, and then plunged, a whirling mass of arms and legs, straight on top of Miss Wilson, who had paused to watch the delicate operation.

A chorus of shrieks rose at this, and several people rushed to the rescue. Jo was pulled off the mistress, who had received the head-girl's full weight in her chest and was temporarily winded. The sight of the austere Miss Wilson, sitting on the floor, crowing for breath, momentarily paralysed the girls, it was left to Miss Annersley, who had fled back to the group at the sound of the screams, to do anything sensible—none of the rest of the Staff happened to be in the room at the moment—and she promptly drove the crowding girls away, ordered someone to bring a glass of water, helped her friend to a chair, and seated her near a window. Meanwhile, Joey was surrounded by her helpers, all anxiously asking where she was hurt. Only Gillian was not there, she sensibly considering that her first duty was to secure the chimney in case it should fall and add to the trouble. By the time she was able to jump down and come out of the cottage, Miss Wilson had recovered her breath, and the deeply embarrassed Jo had managed to convince her followers that she had neither broken nor sprained anything. All she had done was to bruise one knee.

Miss Wilson sipped her water and gradually recovered, while the excited girls sheered off, and drifted back to work. Finally, only Jo and her helpers were left near, and they all stood silent, not quite knowing what to say or do.

"Well," said the science mistress when she could speak, "you'd better get on with that job, hadn't you? It must be nearly time for Kaffee und Kuchen.—As for you Jo, I suppose your bones are *not* made of cast-iron, but I must say you feel uncommonly like it!"

"I—I hope I didn't hurt you much, Miss Wilson?" stammered Jo, for once thoroughly minus the wind in her sails. "I—I—"

"Only winded me, though I still feel sore. But what I wish to know, Joey," continued the ruthless Miss Wilson, "is why you have such a grudge against me?"

"Miss *Wilson!*" gasped Jo, more taken aback than anyone had ever seen her since her early Middle-school days. "I—I—"

"For," went on "Bill" solemnly, though there was a wicked twinkle in her eye, though Jo was too embarrassed to see it, "it certainly looks like it. In the summer you abused me roundly when you fell into the pit when we were in camp. Now you try to extinguish me altogether by falling on me."

Jo didn't know where to look. She decided to face the mistress. What she saw in the face before her suddenly reassured her. "Miss Wilson!" she cried resentfully. "You've been pulling my leg!"

"Well," said Miss Wilson placidly as she took the handful of hairpins Cornelia brought her—her hair had come down in the fall—"*you* tried to rob me of my breath. It's only a fair exchange, I think."

"You had better go and put up your hair again if you feel all right now," said Miss Annersley hastily. "Jo, you must leave that other chimney alone. It can be taken back to its place. Are you sure the other one is quite safe?"

"Oh, yes, Miss Annersley," said Gillian. "I've clipped it on quite firmly."

Miss Annersley mentally resolved to send Eigen and Andreas round to make sure that all erections were safe while the girls were at Kaffee und Kuchen, but she said nothing about that now. "Very good," she replied to Gillian. Then she raised her voice, "Girls, you must finish quickly, for you must be ready to set out your goods after Kaffee und Kuchen, and that will be very soon. Clear up all this mess, and leave the room quite tidy.—Now, Miss Wilson, if you are ready, we'll go."

They left the room, and the laughing girls cleared away the mess of leaves and sprays, papers, muslin, tacks, and all the other rubbish that seems to accumulate on these occasions. Ilonka and Luise carried the second chimney back to the acting-cupboard, and when the gong sounded to call them all to Kaffee und Kuchen, the room was tidy.

"*You're* a nice girl!" the Sixth told Jo afterwards in the privacy of their own form-room. "Even if you *don't* love Bill's lessons, there's no need to try to murder her!"

"I didn't!" protested Jo. Then she stopped and began to laugh.

"What is the joke?" asked Marie.

"Just that I believe this is the one and only time since she came to the School that anyone's succeeded in completely suppressing Bill!"

CHAPTER SIX

THE SALE OF WORK

THE next day saw the Chalet School seething with excitement. Early in the morning the Saints came across the finish up any odds and ends there might be left to do. When all was ready, they took a tour of the whole place, and the noise the two schools and the Chalet Annexe made is indescribable. Only one place was forbidden them, and that was the Magic Cave, which was in charge of Miss Eliott and Mademoiselle Berné, the music and French mistresses at St Scholastika's, who had locked the doors of the salon, and taken the keys. When two or three bright people suddenly bethought them of the entrance through the conservatory, and rushed into the garden, they found that locked also, and the windows completely obscured by dark green curtains.

"How jolly mean!" said Cornelia disappointedly.

"*Who* is mean?" demanded Hilary Burn, one of the Fifth Form Saints.

"Your folk for taking the key and then stopping us from seeing through here," Cornelia told her. "Isn't this *your* stunt, by the way? You might tell us what it's all about."

"Got Charlotte Yonge's books in your library?" asked Hilary detachedly.

"Not an earthly," was the calm reply. "Jo could tell you."

"Jo could tell her what?" asked Jo herself, coming on them from the lawn, where she had been satisfying herself that the clock-golf was quite ready and that Elsie and Evadne, who were to be in charge of it, knew how to explain it adequately.

"Have we any books by—*who* did you say?" asked Cornelia, turning to Hilary.

"Charlotte Yonge," replied Hilary in rather more respectful tones than she had hitherto used. Hilary stood in wholesome awe of the Chalet School head-girl.

"Yes; we have some," said Jo. "Why do you want to know?"

"It isn't me—it's Corney," explained Hilary.

"Corney?" Jo stared, for at no time was Cornelia much of a reader. "What's at the back of all this?"

"Well, I be gum-swizzled!" ejaculated the indignant Cornelia. "She asked me, and I said you could tell her. I guess she's gone batty."

"You asked me about the Magic Cave," said Hilary with dancing eyes.

"What on earth has Charlotte Yonge to do with that?" asked Jo, now thoroughly puzzled.

"Only that we got the idea out of one of her books," explained Hilary.

"Which one? I've read a good many of them —the historical ones, at any rate, and I don't remember anything about Magic Caves in them."

"This is historical. It's the one called *The Three Brides*. It was Elspeth's idea in the beginning. She read the book at Christmas, and thought it would be rather a good idea for the Sale. So she brought it back with her, and honestly, we were all thrilled. You'll pay so much —a schilling, I believe—and then you get a prize, as well as all the fun."

"We haven't got *The Three Brides*," said Jo thoughtfully. "We have the historical ones like *A Reputed Changeling*, and *The Chaplet of Pearls*, and *The Dove in the Eagle's Nest*. But we haven't gone in for any of her contemporary tales except the *Daisy Chain*; of course, and *Pillars of the House*. I must see about getting some of the others. They are all nice, I know. And goodness knows, no one could pick up slang from *her*!" she added with an infectious grin.

"But," complained Cornelia at this point, "if we haven't got it, how under the canopy am I to find out about the Magic Cave?"

"You can't. That was the great idea," said Hilary calmly.

Jo chuckled at this, and went off, leaving the highly indignant Cornelia to settle with her friend in her own way, and obligingly closing her ears for once as the opening sentence floated after her: "Of all the mean, flubdub, left-footed *gumps*—"

She did stop to call back, "You be careful who hears you, Corney!" but that was all she did, and Hilary Burn was subsequently in a position to inform her own crowd that Corney Flower's language was an eye-opener, once she was fairly started.

At noon the Saints went back to their own abode for Mittagessen, a rest, and to change their costumes for the afternoon. The Chalet School went in for their own meal with un-impaired appetites, in spite of all the excitement prevailing. After Mittagessen, they were very indignant when they were all despatched to their cubicles with orders to lie down on their beds and stay there till they heard the bell. Mademoiselle knew that some of them were already screwed up to the highest pitch, and she did not want any outbursts of weeping. They went with many grumbles, for they were also forbidden to talk. However, once they were settled, the quiet, after the busy morning they had had, worked its usual spell, and a good many of them went to sleep; while even those who didn't were greatly calmed and refreshed.

At fourteen the bell sounded, and they all jumped up and proceeded to dress for their parts. As it was a Fairy-Tale Bazaar, the girls were to assume the characters of the old fairy-tales. The Robin made a delightful little Prince, with blue tunic and cap, and short mantle over one shoulder. Amy Stevens wore a full witch's dress, pointed hat, broomstick and all. Simone Lecoutier was another witch. Marie von Eschenau made a charming Beauty, with big Louise Redfield, an American girl in the Sixth Form, for the Beast, though Louise had flatly refused to spend the afternoon in the Beast's mask, having had experience of it before. Jo, whose cropped black hair always caused her to be in constant demand for male characters, was the Prince for Snowdrop, clad in crimson slashed with cream. Gillian Linton, possessor of the authentic colouring of Snowdrop herself, was the Princess, all in white. Louise Rotheim was the wicked Stepmother, and the Seven Little Men were Cornelia, Joyce, Hilda, Olga, Ilonka, Maria, Lilli, and were all clad in green, with long beards fixed to their pointed caps. They looked very well, and as both Jo and Gillian were a good head taller than any of them, they made a most effective group.

The Saints had elected to represent Bluebeard, and Gipsy Carson was the wicked tyrant with a huge horsehair beard dyed blue, and a magnificent turban. Hilda Wilmot was Fatima; Maisie Gomm, a pretty, somewhat empty-headed girl of seventeen, was Sister Anne, and Elspeth Macdonald was the faithful Hassan. Simone's stall was attended by Vanna di Ricci as the Sleeping Beauty, with trails of briar-roses twined about her, and Margia Stevens as the Prince. The rest of the Upper Fifth were there, also having been brought in as various palace characters. The remainder of the Sixth and Lower Fifth were in attendance on the refreshments, where the cakes and sweets would also be sold, and wore garments that seemed to fit in with the rest, so that Goody Two-shoes might bring your coffee, and Dick Whittington would try to persuade you to buy marrons glacés. All the Juniors were clustered round the Wishing-Well, clad as fairies—there were twenty-two fairy-dresses of their size in the acting-cupboard—and those of the Fourth and Third who were to give the dancing display, wore their simple, short-waisted, long-skirted frocks, which fitted in delightfully with the rest of the characters. The rest had been assigned to posts as door-keepers and so on.

The Fifth Form of St Scholastika's were to help with the Magic Cave, Miss Elliott and Mademoiselle Berné having reserved to themselves the places of "unseen musicians." They all wore Eastern draperies, with the exceptions of Ida Reaveley and Nancy Wilmot, the two biggest among them, who were got up in full Turkish male costume, and Hilary, who was to be the Peri, and whose floating garments were hung with strings of beads to such an extent that she vowed she felt like a walking jeweller's-shop!

"I say! They're coming!" called out Elsie Carr, darting in from the garden where she and Evadne, with two of the Fourth to take money at the gate, had been arranging clubs and balls in readiness for the clock-golf. "There's about twenty coming from the 'Kron Prinz Karl'; and at least fifty from the other side."

"Frieda—Frieda!" called Jo across the hall to where Frieda, in flowing white draperies, with the wonderful golden mantle of her hair falling round her, was seated on the edge of the metamorphosed mistress's platform as the Good Fairy of the Well. "Are all your people ready?"

102

"Quite as ready as yours, and so *much* more quiet!" returned the Fairy with emphasis; and Jo subsided, duly squashed, for her Seven Little Men were chattering from sheer excitement like so many magpies.

Then the doors opened, and the crowds poured in. At fifteen o'clock, Mademoiselle led a little procession on to the prettily decorated platform at the head of the hall, and the girls all looked eagerly at the thin, scholarly Bishop, whom many of them were seeing for the first time.

The chair was taken by the local dignitary, the Baron von und zu Wertheimer, a young man in his early twenties, who had officiated at school celebrations before, and who could, as wicked Jo said, be relied on not to spend too long on speechifying. Indeed, he said even less than that young lady had anticipated. He called on Dr Russell to read out the report on the free wards at the Sanatorium, introduced the Bishop as briefly as he could, and then sat down. The Bishop, too, was merciful, and after talking for seven minutes about the great work which the Sanatorium and its devoted servants were, under God, performing, he declared the Sale of Work open, and wished it every success.

Amidst tumultuous cheers from the girls, the two youngest members of the two schools—Yolanda di Maladetta and Marjorie Burn—were hoisted up on to the platform, and trotted up to him to hand him the fountain-pen the girls offered for his acceptance. They were followed by the Robin as head of the Annexe, who had been chosen to present a bouquet to Mademoiselle Lepâttre, and little Ailsa Macdonald from St Scholastika's, with a similar offering for Miss Browne. Then votes of thanks were offered, and the real business of the afternoon began.

With wild bounds, the girls fled to their own particular posts, the Chalet Fourths and Thirds hurrying to get ready for the dancing, and those people with outside work hastening to take their places.

Jo and Luise disappeared into their cottage, while Snowdrop stood at the door; the Seven Little Men clustered round her, and the other girls grouped themselves as picturesquely as they could. The Bishop, having left the platform, whither a small orchestra was making its way "to charm the savage breast and make it yield up its cash," as Jo remarked, began a tour of the stalls. He had a genial word for everyone, and paused to chat with those girls whom he had met at the wedding of Frieda's sister, Bernhilda. Greatly to the joy of the Chalet School Juniors, he went to the Wishing-Well first, and demanded a "present for a *good* boy."

"I am that, eh, Frieda?" he said with a smile at his pretty niece.

Frieda laughed up at him. "Are you so sure, Uncle? Well, the Frog Prince must see what he can do for you.—Lower the bucket, Princess."

The Princess, Yolanda di Maladetta, lowered the canvas bucket carefully, and demanded, "If you please, Prince Frog, a present for a good—

bo—bishop!" Whereupon the Bishop chuckled.

There was a pause, and then a somewhat muffled voice said, "I reckon that's done it this time.—Haul away, Princess!" with an unexpectedly American accent, for the Prince was little Marie Varick, whose mother was slowly dying up at the Sonnalpe, though Marie, of course, had no idea of that.

The Princess hauled, and when the bucket reached the top of the well one of the fairies made haste to take out the parcel and hand it to the great man with a funny little bob intended for a bow.

Frieda saw it and only just suppressed a wail of remonstrance. She had devoted nearly an hour the day before to teaching Wanda von der Kock to bow prettily. The Bishop smiled, and patted the straight brown locks of the fairy before he opened his parcel.

"Oh, I do so hope it isn't a pen!" breathed Faithful John who was standing near.

It was not a pen. When his lordship had got it undone, it turned out to be a parti-coloured stick of candy.

"It is a really good one, isn't it?" observed the Frog Prince who had climbed out to see what it was.

"It is very good indeed," said the Bishop gravely. "You have made a neat choice."

"I reckon it'll be a help when you write your next sermon," said the Prince with equal gravity. "Seems as if you get so much more done when you've something handy to suck."

The Bishop nearly choked over a chuckle, and after another word or two, passed on to Beauty and the Beast. Here he had a chat with Marie and Simone, both of whom he knew, and then proceeded to invest in hem-stitched handkerchiefs.

He left them, and went on, pausing at each stall, till, when at length he reached the cottage of Snowdrop and her satellites, he was laden with parcels of all sizes and shapes, some of them coming undone, for the excited girls had not packed them properly.

"Let me have those put together for you, my lord," said Joey from one of the "windows." "They are all dropping out. What an advertisement for the Guides!—Here, Lonny, get some paper and string and make them into a respectable package, won't you?"

The Bishop thankfully resigned his purchases to Ilonka, who bore them off, and presently returned them all securely fastened, and packed into a bass bag she had discovered somewhere.

"And now," said the Bishop when he had thanked her, and was watching Jo tuck in the china and puzzles he had added to his shopping, "this is the last of the stalls. What ought I to do next?"

Jo meditated. "There's the Magic Cave—but that might wait.—What is the time, someone?—Oh, then, Monsignor, I think you had better go and take your seat for the folk-dance display.—Corney! Take Monsignor along, will you, and see that he gets a good seat. It's due to begin in ten minutes now."

"And when it is over, may I not have the pleasure of escorting you to the Magic Cave?" he asked her, laughing. "And Snowdrop and the Witchwife too?"

"Oh, thank you," said Jo. "That will be awfully jolly. Won't you leave your things here till you come back, Monsignor? Then you needn't worry about them."

He left the bag in her charge, and went off in Cornelia's wake to enjoy the dancing, while the girls turned back to attend to their customers who were now thronging round them. For the next hour or so they were kept very busy, and the bag into which the proceeds were put soon grew heavy. Jo seized a moment's breathing-space to rush out and see how the clock-golf was getting on, for it had been her suggestion, and she was anxious about it. She was met by Elsie and Evadne with beaming faces. The fathers and brothers who had ventured to the Sale with their womenfolk had been thankful to find it, and were enjoying themselves hugely.

"*Thought* it would appeal to them!" quoth Jo; and departed to find the Bishop had left a message that he was waiting for her at the door to the Magic Cave. She made sure that everything was quite all right, and then departed for the salon, where she found him surrounded by a motley throng of characters from the fairy-tales.

"We are all going to see the Magic Cave," he told her as she came up. "This is my—

how do you say it in England?—I am inviting you."

"You mean it's your treat," said Jo. "How awfully good of you, Monsignor."

He laughed, and led them in to the doors of the conservatory, whence issued strains of music played by a violin and piano, while at the doors stood the two turbaned figures who were Ida and Nancy in everyday life, but who now looked simply gigantic with their high-piled turbans, and anything but English with their browned skins, flashing teeth, and huge brass curtain-rings tied to their ears.

"The Bishop first!" cried Jo eagerly.

The two figures salaamed low to him, and a voice sang softly from the Cave:

> "Hush! The Peri's cave is near,
> No one enters scatheless here;
> Lightly tread and lowly bend,
> Win the Peri for your friend."

At the same time, Ida advanced on him with a folded band of muslin which she tied over his eyes, and then a graceful Eastern lady appeared, caught his hand, and led him inside, and the doors were shut. Suddenly, shrill blasts of a whistle broke out, and then there came the clapping of hands and shouts of laughter.

"Oh, I wish they'd hurry up!" said Jo impatiently. "I'm simply longing to see what it is—and we'll have *The Three Brides* added to the library next term," she added with decision.

One by one they all passed inside, and again and again those left heard the shouts of laughter and became more and more anxious for their turn. Finally, it was her turn. She was bidden advance, and while the song rang out, Nancy blindfolded her. Then she felt her hand taken, and was led on between the rows of sweet-smelling flowers. Again the chorus rang out, and even as she made a low bow in obedience to the command, the whistle blast sounded just behind her. With an exclamation, Jo swung round, only to hear it behind her again, while something seemed to be tugging at her. She spun round once more, and then again, and with the final twist came on disaster, for the foil slung from her left hip got between her legs, so that she sprawled ignominiously, face downwards, on the tiled floor, where her groping hand shot out and grasped someone's ankle in a grip that drew a squeal from its owner. At once the bandage was whipped off, and she found herself lying at full length in front of Hilary Burn, and clutching at her foot as if it were a rope flung to a drowning man.

Somewhat embarrassed, Jo scrambled to her feet, aware that the Bishop and all who had preceded her were rocking with laughter over her confusion. Then she found that a string had been attached to her sword belt, and tugged at it sharply, expecting to find the annoying whistle at the end. To her amazement it was not there; but she found instead a pretty little brooch of gold twisted wire, surrounding a small Roman pearl.

"Am I to keep this?" she asked doubtfully.

The only answer was another song from behind the tall palms which had all been massed together across one corner:

"Away, away! No longer stay.
Others come to join our play!"

So she laughingly slipped aside to join the throng behind the Peri and watch the next-comer, even as Hilary, before she settled herself again, remarked, "Well, everyone has bowed to me so far. But Jo is the only one who has prostrated herself."

Gillian was the last, and she, like Jo, stumbled, this time over her unaccustomed long skirts, and only the outstretched hand of one of the genii who were in attendance on the Peri saved her from complete bouleversement.

"Your party don't seem very steady on their feet, Joey," said Gipsy Carson, who had been one of the first there. "First you, and now Snowdrop!"

"It's the sight of your beard, Bluebeard," retorted Jo. "It's enough to give anyone nightmare for a week on end!"

"You'll have to go now," said the Peri, as she shifted her position with a sigh. "I believe there are crowds outside, and this place is getting like an oven!"

They slipped out into the garden through the doors which the genii politely held open for them, thus giving the poor Peri a breath of sadly needed fresh air at the same time. Then the Bishop went off to try his hand at clock-golf, and the stall-holders suddenly remembered their duties and fled back to them.

At six o'clock—eighteen, by Middle Europe time—the variety entertainment opened, and the bazaar part of the affair was deserted, and everyone crowded in to be accommodated on backless forms, where they listened to choruses, solos, recitations, and dialogues. "Plato," the School's somewhat eccentric singing-master, exhibited some wonderful feats of conjuring, and Biddy O'Ryan, clad in little short skirt and shawl, with bare feet, and her splendid hair hanging loose over her shoulders, executed an Irish jig that nearly brought the house down.

The wind-up of it was a chorus and dance by the entire company. Jo sang the solo, her lovely voice being always in demand on these occasions, and all went well till they linked arms for a kind of breakdown.

It *was* a breakdown, though not quite what they had intended. For as they careered from the back to the front of the platform, it was felt to shake ominously. The performers were far too much excited to notice it. With a stamp they all turned right, and pranced along for three steps. Then they turned with another stamp which sounded like thunder on the hollow boards. They prepared to prance left; but the stage had had enough of it. Unable to bear up any longer, it collapsed amidst clouds of dust and to the accompaniment of wild yells.

Luckily, no one was hurt, and once the audience was assured of that, they simply held their sides with laughing. It only ended when the dust-choked orchestra rose to their feet, and with a fine, resonant chord, struck up the old German chorale, "Nun danket alle Gott," which had been adopted as one of the School songs. With full throats everyone sang it; and then the girls sang the other School song. "You'll Get There!" and if many of the audience were unable to understand the words, the spirit of the song must have got through to them.

After that, people began to gather up their parcels, and to say good-bye, and the long queues which had led *into* the Chalet in the afternoon, now led *out* of it.

Abendessen came next, and after that was over—and a most hilarious meal it was—they returned to the Hall where they settled down to count up their gains. It had certainly *seemed* a very successful afternoon, but they could not be sure until they knew their total.

Three times the members of each stall or entertainment added up their money before they brought it to Mademoiselle Lepâttre and Miss Browne (who, with Miss Soames and Miss Leslie, were sitting at a big table in the Speisesaal) to find out the final total. Three times was this added up by the four before it was announced. Then—there was a dead silence as Mademoiselle, as the Head of the longer established school, rose and gave it out. When the girls heard it there came such a burst of cheering as must have been heard nearly down to Spärtz. For the proceeds were almost treble the highest sum they had ever made before, and Mademoiselle held out hopes that this year they might be able to support yet another bed.

"How simply gorgeous!" said Jo joyously. "This has been the nicest Sale we've ever had, and it certainly is the best from the point of view of money. Three che—" Her voice suddenly trailed off into silence, as her eyes caught a movement at the door.

Dr Jem stood there, his face very grave, his keen eyes searching the serried ranks of the girls. Jo said afterwards that her heart stood still. Her brother-in-law had left the Sale early, and had returned to the Sonnalpe, and she knew that only bad news could have brought him back like this. Her mind flew to little Marie Varick; but even as she looked round for the child, the doctor's voice sounded.

"Gillian—Joyce!" he said. "I want you at once."

With a spring, Gillian was at his side, her long gown held up, her hand pushing back her long black hair impatiently from her face. Joyce was struggling to get at him from the crowd where she had been standing. Silence had fallen, for they all guessed that something was very badly wrong. Joey followed them, anxious to help if she could. The four left the room, even as Mademoiselle hurried after them.

Later on that night, the Chalet girls knew that Mrs Linton was very ill—dying, the doctors feared—and Gillian and Joyce had been taken up to the Sonnalpe to see her—most likely, to say good-bye.

CHAPTER SEVEN

ALL'S WELL!

IN the quiet room at the Sonnalpe there was a great hush. The slim-black-haired girl with eyes like blue pansies sat watching the still occupant of the narrow white bed as if there was nothing and nobody else in the whole world. By the bedside sat Dr James Russell, and behind him stood Dr Jack Maynard, his most trusted assistant. A white-clad, white-capped nurse stood at the other side, and the eyes of all three were on the patient, who lay there so quietly that it almost seemed as if she had ceased to breathe.

Three days had passed since the day of the Sale—the day when they had all been so happy at school, and their happiness had been cut short by the abrupt summons of Gillian and Joyce Linton to their mother. During those days, the doctors and nurses had fought death with every means at their command. Sometimes they seemed to be gaining the battle; sometimes it seemed as if they must lose it; sometimes, as now it appeared to be a drawn affair. Mrs Linton was still living, but that was all that could be said.

When the doctor had called the girls, he had told them that there was heart trouble which had caused this sudden collapse. No one could account for it. That afternoon, Mrs Linton, whose bed had been wheeled out on to the balcony of her room, had been better than she had been since she had entered the Sanatorium. Her nurse had left her to bring the milk and sponge-cakes which formed her afternoon meal, and had returned to find her lying back on her pillows with grey face and blue lips. They had worked madly on her, but never once since that moment had she fully recovered consciousness.

"A shock," said Dr Jem in answer to Gillian's questions. "We have no idea at present what it was. She had no letters, and, so far as we can find out, no visitors. When she wakes up and is fitter we'll hear all about it, I expect. But she is terribly ill now. Yes, Gill; you shall be with her. But you must be very quiet and self-controlled, whatever happens."

Gillian thanked him gratefully. She was too inexperienced to know that he only allowed the two girls to be so constantly with their mother during the day because he feared that there was no hope of recovery. Joyce, even more ignorant than she, thought her mother sleeping, and hoped that when this long slumber was ended she would wake much better and stronger.

The School had broken up since then, and Joey had arrived at the Sonnalpe that day, together with Maria Marani who was to spend the week with her sister. Frieda had gone home to Innsbruck to greet her new-born nephew, but Giovanna and Anita Rincini had joined their cousin, now Signora di Bersetti, though very little changed from the Bette Rincini who had been such a tower of strength to the Chalet School in its early days.

During the night, Gillian and Joyce slept in a little room not far from their mother's, for the doctor would not allow them to be deprived of their sleep. But in the daytime, they spent nearly all their time in that white room. Joyce had left it only half an hour before, sent out by the doctor to get some exercise. Gillian he had been unable to move. She acquiesced to Joyce's going, but she remained herself.

"I'm not going," she said quietly. "Jo will see to Joyce, I know. I can't leave Mummy just now. When she's better—oh yes; I'll go for walks then. But while she's like this, I *can't*!"

Dr Jem looked at her sharply. What he saw in her pretty face made him let her alone. He reflected somewhat sadly that in all probability the time was near at hand when the girl would be glad to think that she had sat thus with her mother during those last hours.

As the four sat watching, there was a little stir from the bed, and all were on the alert at once. Gillian rose from the chair near the foot of the bed where she had been sitting, and bent over her mother lovingly. The doctor slipped his fingers down the thin wrist to feel the pulse that was beating there so feebly that for a moment he thought it had ceased.

"Careful, Gill!" he said very softly.

The warning was necessary. Tears had brimmed Gillian's eyes for the first time during those awful three days, and but for his word, she would have sobbed aloud. But once more she pulled herself together, and stooped down so that he lips were at the ear so long deaf to everything.

"Mummy!" she said gently. "It's Gill. Won't you wake up?"

For a minute or two there was no response. Then a low moan came from the pale lips. "Oh, Joyce—my litle Joyce!"

At once Dr Maynard slipped out of the room to seek the child. He knew that she and Joey were only playing tennis on the hard court which had been laid for the use of the nurses, and he brought her back very quickly. Jo came with them, for Joyce clung to her childishly.

By this time there could be no doubt that Mrs Linton was rousing out of the heavy stupor, though whether she was coming back to consciousness or fever, no one could say yet. Her eyes remained fast closed, and she paid no heed to Gillian's tender whispers.

"My baby!" she moaned as the young man and the two schoolgirls entered the room. "Oh, my little Joyce! Expelled!"

At the words, Joyce's face whitened, and she shrank back against Jo, who flung an arm round her. Gillian was speaking now, in her low, soft tones. "Oh no, Mummy! She isn't expelled—indeed she isn't! It's Thekla who has been expelled. Joyce is all right, and doing well at school now."

But the sick woman paid no heed. The heart-rending moans went on, and every now and then they could catch broken murmurs about Joyce and expulsion.

It was plain now to the doctors what had caused this sudden collapse. Mrs Linton must have heard someone talking of the latest doings at the Chalet School—scarcely a surprising thing when one remembers the number of patients who had daughters there—and the awful shock of Joyce's supposed expulsion was quite enough to have brought on this.

Dr Jem's jaw set like a ramrod as he inwardly cursed the heedless gossip which had done this. Jo was wishing that she could have had a quiet ten minutes alone with Thekla von Stift.

"It's all *her* fault this has happened," she thought as she held Joyce tightly to her, trying to give the child courage by contact with herself. Then she spoke aloud. "Joyce, go and tell your mother it's all right, mein Vögelein! Perhaps she'll hear you and wake up properly."

Terrified, almost heart-broken, Joyce stumbled up to the bedside. "Mummy!" she said piteously. "Oh, Mummy, I'm not expelled—hand of honour, I'm not! Wake up, Mummy dearest! It's your own little Joycie!"

But Mrs Linton did not hear the words, nearly choked as they were with sobs. She seemed to be relapsing into her former state of coma, and the doctors knew that if this happened, only a miracle could save her. Already they had pushed the girls aside, and, with nurse ably backing them up, were once more in the thick of the battle. Gillian came round the bed, and was standing holding one of Joyce's hands. The poor silly child was undergoing the bitterest pain she had ever known, and even the grip of her elder sister was no comfort to her.

"Oh, *make* her wake up!" she cried. "Oh, I'll be so good if only she wakes up! Tell her, Gill! —Jo, *you* tell her!"

"Hush, Joyce!" said the doctor sharply. "If you make a noise—" Then he broke off, for Jo, releasing herself from Joyce's hot clutch, had come to the bedside, and was wriggling past him.

"Let me, Jem!" she said. "My voice is clearer than either of theirs—and anyway, if she's as ill as all that, it isn't like to make much difference."

The doctors realised that. They had administered powerful stimulants, and could only wait and see if they would take effect. Jem Russell made room for his young sister-in-law, his fingers still on that barely beating pulse, his eyes searching the grey face for signs of renewed life.

Joey knelt down, her face just above the one on the pillow. For a moment she was silent as she flung all her energy into a frantic prayer. Then she spoke in her normally clear, bell-like tones. "Mrs Linton! Who on earth told you that rigmarole? There isn't a word of truth in it! You wake up and listen to me, and I'll tell you the *real* tale."

It was certainly the last thing anyone had expected. Jo's voice was as ordinary as if she were talking to one of the Middles. Perhaps there was even a little more head-girl authority in it. At any rate, where all else had failed, it began to succeed. Mrs Linton's lashes quivered, and though she didn't lift them, the doctor, on the alert at once, acted promptly. Shoving Jo aside so unceremoniously that she fell sprawling, he put a teaspoonful of the powerful stimulant he had been using between the pale lips, saying quietly, "Drink this, Mrs Linton, at once, if you please."

Unmistakably she swallowed, and then he stepped back. "Tell her again, Joey—Joyce, come here!"

Joyce crept to his side, thankfully giving him her hand which he held in a firm grip, while Jo, on her mettle despite a bruised shoulder, once more spoke. "Mrs Linton!" It was the complete head-girl now. "Will you please wake *at once* and listen to me! Joyce has not been expelled! She is quite safe, and quite all right."

This time, success followed the effort. The stimulant was doing its work. Already the pulse, fluttering uncertainly in the wrist, was growing stronger, and the grey pallor was leaving the face. Once more the long lashes fluttered, and this time they lifted, showing the blue eyes so like Joyce's.

"Joyce, come here!" said Jo imperatively. Joyce came at once, and Jo, with one arm round her, told the tale in a few bold words. "Here's Joyce herself. She's all right. Some one has been telling you a pack of lies. She isn't expelled, and she isn't going to be! I never heard such poppy-cock in my life!"

A faint smile quivered on the pale lips at the Americanism. Jem Russell slipped an arm under the pillow and raised the patient's head slightly. "Drink this, Mrs Linton," he said, holding a medicine-glass to her lips.

Mrs Linton drank, her eyes fixed all the time on Jo, who, with Joyce and Gillian on either side of her, was engaged in willing the invalid to pull back up the slope. Suddenly she relaxed her efforts. "Tell her it's all right, you little ninny!" she said fiercely to Joyce, giving the child a slight shake as she did so.

Obediently Joyce did so. "I'm not expelled, Mummy, and I'm not going to be. Hand of honour, it's all right!"

Urged to it by a shake from the watchful Jo, Gillian added her quota. "It's just as Jo says, Mummy. Joyce isn't expelled. She isn't going to be, and she's got a decent report."

The blue eyes slowly showed comprehension, but Mrs Linton was still too near death to speak or move. The nurse gave her an injection, and again there was silence. But presently the white lips moved, though they had thought that never again would they do so in this world. Gillian, leaning close, caught the whisper.

"Darlings—is this holidays?"

The girl nodded. Then she managed to control herself sufficiently to reply. "Yes; only a week, though, so hurry up and get better, for we want to talk. We've such lots of jolly things to tell you."

A faint smile came. Then the heavy lids fell again, but it was in natural sleep, and not that terrible coma. Dr Jem made a swift examination, then he nodded. "Stay for the next hour, will you, Jack?—Girls, you come with me."

Obediently they followed him out of the room, and along the corridor to the room the Lintons had been using. Arrived there, he made them sit down before he said anything. Then he spoke. "Children, I think we have a good chance now of pulling her through. Stay here for the present, and I'll come back in an hour and tell you how she is.—Jo, I'm going to send you folk something to eat, and it is to be eaten—mind that! Otherwise, nobody goes back to that room to-night." Then he vanished.

An hour later he came back with good news. Mrs Linton had fallen asleep and was appreciably stronger. The three girls were to go to "Die Rosen," where they were to go to bed, and they were to stay in bed till he gave them permission to get up. If there should be any change at all before then, he would see that they knew.

Gillian would have liked to dispute this, but she was too worn out by what she had endured during the past three days to find strength for it. Dr Mensch came with the car, and drove them the short distance to "Die Rosen," where they were met on the doorstep by Madge Russell, who marched them all off to bed, saw them safely between the sheets, and then dosed them all with hot milk. Gillian's held something else, for the doctor knew that the reaction would most likely keep her awake, and she had had as much as she could stand. Jo and Joyce needed nothing. Joyce's lashes fell almost before she handed back the milk-mug, and Jo cuddled down with a yawn and a murmured "O-oh! How done I am!" and was asleep like a baby. But the doctor's wife never left Gillian's side till she saw that she, too, was safely over.

It was noon of next day before Gillian roused out of that deep sleep, and then Joyce and Joey were there, waiting to tell her the good news that her mother had turned the corner, and, though she was still not out of danger, yet she was slowly and surely making her way back to life again.

"Of course, it's all thanks to you, Joey!"

It was a week later, and Mrs Linton had been having a tea-party consisting of her own two girls and Jo Bettany. They had been out on the balcony, and if the patient still looked very frail, there was about her an air of returning strength that thrilled those who loved her with happiness. Gillian was leading the way home after they had been dismissed, and now she stopped suddenly to turn and fling this remark at Jo. As that young lady, who was immediately behind her, had not expected the stop, she promptly fell over her leader, and the pair rolled on the ground together.

"The next time you intend to stop pointblank, Gillian Linton, I'll be grateful if you'll give me due notice!" said Jo when she had got to her feet again. "It's as well it's been fine the last few days, or a nice mess we'd both be in with the horrible chalky clay there is about here."

"I'm sorry," apologised Gillian. "I didn't mean to upset you. Really, I was only trying to thank you for all you've done for us."

"Rubbish!" said Jo. "All I did was to speak properly. Jem says so. He says if you'd only spoken out and bossed your mother as I did—well, she's getting on all right now," she concluded lamely.

But Gillian stuck to her point. "All the same, Joey, you did save Mummy's life for us, and we can never be grateful enough."

"Well, don't talk nonsense to me about it—that's all I ask!" said Jo ungraciously. She hated being thanked, and she really had no idea what to say in reply. "Are you coming down to school to-morrow, by the way, or does Jem intend to keep you up here a bit longer?"

"We're staying over the week-end, but after that we're to come down as usual," said Gillian. "Stacie is to come down with us—isn't it splendid that she can walk now?—and I don't suppose we'll come up for a fortnight after that."

"And anyway," struck in Joyce, "I want to do a little work and get settled in. This will be such a short term—and I do seem to have such an awful lot to make up," she added with a sigh.

"Oh, you'll soon do that," said Jo, thankful that the conversation had left her own doings. "You've got plenty of brains, and now that you're going to use them, you'll soon find that you get on as well as anyone."

Joyce, whose term-end report had shown her as second-bottom in the Lower Fifth, nodded. The events of the last few months had made a very great change in her, and the spoilt, selfish little piece of indolence who had come to the Chalet School after Christmas had gone, never to return again. She knew that she would have to work hard, but she felt that it would be something she could do for Joey, and Joyce almost adored Joey now. As for Gillian, she had always been a worker, but, as Madge Russell had gently pointed out to her, she had tried to make Joyce's life far too easy, and had helped to spoil the younger girl. Now she was beginning to let her stand on her own feet, and though it would be some time before she gave up worrying herself unduly about her sister's welfare, still she was more or less prepared to leave her to work out her own salvation. Incidentally, Gillian was losing her care worn look, and becoming more girlish than she had been for the last two or three years.

"Altogether," said Jo, as she tossed a pebble over the edge and watched it strike against a tree-stump and bounce off again at a tangent, "things might have been worse this term."

"Next term will be your last," said Gillian, standing beside her. "What are you going to do then—go to the University?"

Jo shook her head. "No; if I go away at all, it'll be to Belsornia to be lady-in-waiting to

Elisaveta. But I don't think it's very likely—not with all the babies we have about the place now. No; I think I shall probably just stay at home and help my sister with David and Sybil and the twins. And I shall go on with my singing, of course. And then I want to write books."

"You'll have plenty to do at that rate," said Gillian.

Joyce looked wide-eyed at her idol. "Write books? Oh, how *wonderful* that will be! Do be quick and write the first one, Joey! Then we can all swank about knowing an authoress!"

"You'll have to wait a bit yet," grinned the would-be-authoress. "It's to write, yet. And then it'll probably go the rounds of all the publishers and none of them may appreciate it."

"Oh, of course they will!" said Joyce quickly.

Gillian looked at the head-girl with mischief in her eyes. "Fancy you an authoress, Joey! Well, when that happens, you'll *have* to grow up, of course!"

"Never!" said Jo with decision as she turned away and led them up the road to "Die Rosen" and Kaffee und Kuchen.

MILL GREEN

School Series

by Alison Prince

Now there's a great new school series in Armada.

Mill Green is a big, new comprehensive – with more than its fair share of dramas and disasters! Get to know Matt, Danny, Rachel, and the rest of the First Form mob in their first two exciting adventures.

Mill Green on Fire
When someone starts fires in the school and blames the caretaker, Matt is determined to catch the real culprit. But his brilliant plan to catch the firebug goes horribly wrong . . .

Mill Green on Stage
The First Formers prepare for the Christmas pantomime – and sparks soon fly when Marcia Mudd, a ghastly new girl, gets the best part. But when Matt locks Marcia in a cupboard and she disappears from the school, there's big trouble for everyone . . .

More stories about Mill Green will be published in Armada.

Armada

CAPTAIN ARMADA

HI KIDS! I'VE GOT THE POWER TO BRING YOU FUN, ADVENTURE, AND EXCITEMENT!

Here are just some of the best-selling titles that Armada has to offer:

- ☐ **The Whizzkid's Handbook 2** Peter Eldin 95p
- ☐ **The Vanishing Thieves** Franklin W. Dixon 95p
- ☐ **14th Armada Ghost Book** Mary Danby 85p
- ☐ **The Chalet School and Richenda** Elinor M. Brent-Dyer 95p
- ☐ **The Even More Awful Joke Book** Mary Danby 95p
- ☐ **Adventure Stories** Enid Blyton 85p
- ☐ **Biggles Learns to Fly** Captain W. E. Johns 90p
- ☐ **The Mystery of Horseshoe Canyon** Ann Sheldon 95p
- ☐ **Mill Green on Stage** Alison Prince 95p
- ☐ **The Mystery of the Sinister Scarecrow** Alfred Hitchcock 95p
- ☐ **The Secret of Shadow Ranch** Carolyn Keene 95p

Armadas are available in bookshops and newsagents, but can also be ordered by post.

HOW TO ORDER
ARMADA BOOKS, Cash Sales Dept., GPO Box 29, Douglas, Isle of Man, British Isles. Please send purchase price of book plus postage, as follows:–

    1–4 Books .... 10p per copy
    5 Books or more . . . . no further charge
    25 Books sent post free within U.K.

Overseas Customers: 12p per copy

NAME (Block letters)

———————————————————————

ADDRESS

———————————————————————

———————————————————————